WITHDRAW

BATAVIA PUBLIC LIBRAR

3 6173 00108

D0986902

WITHDRAWN

Batavia Public Library
335 West Wilson
Batavia, Il   60510
879-1393

Library Charges For
Missing Date Card

GAYLORD MG

Killing Words

Also by Diana Ramsay

The Dark Descends
Four Steps to Death

Diana Ramsay

Killing Words

St. Martin's Press New York

This novel is a work of fiction. All of the events, char-
acters, names, and places depicted in this novel are
entirely fictitious or used fictitiously.

KILLING WORDS. Copyright © 1994 by Diana Ramsay.
All rights reserved. Printed in the United States of
America. No part of this book may be used or repro-
duced in any manner whatsoever without written per-
mission except in the case of brief quotations
embodied in critical articles or reviews. For information, address St. Martin's Press, 175 Fifth Avenue,
New York, N.Y. 10010.

Design by Judith A. Stagnitto

Library of Congress Cataloging-in-Publication Data

Ramsay, Diana.
    Killing words / Diana Ramsay.
        p.   cm.
    ISBN 0-312-11015-4 (hardcover)
    1. College teachers' spouses—New England—
Fiction.   2. Women detectives—New England—
Fiction.   I. Title.
PS3568.A449K55   1994
813'.54—dc20   94-1115
                                                CIP

First Edition: July 1994

10 9 8 7 6 5 4 3 2 1

In Memory of Tessa Sayle

Part
One

1

"The principal item on the agenda today is the bake-off for the homeless," Millicent Neumeyer announced, her gruff contralto resounding through the big, multiwindowed room where dances for the students of Northvale College were held; on less festive occasions like today, with the addition of wooden folding chairs, the room became an impromptu lecture hall.

"It is essential—absolutely essential—that we all do the best job of baking we're capable of. That means no Duncan Hines mixes, thank you very much."

Mild laughter from the assembled wives of the Northvale faculty, an appropriate response to a witticism from the wife of the president.

God forbid, Amelia Cunningham thought, that "Betty Crocker" should profane Millicent's lips. Unfair, probably, but who wanted to be fair to Millicent? She was so overpowering, six feet tall and with a broadness in the beam emphasized by the hairy brown tweed skirt and jacket she had on today, plainly hand-loomed and testimony to her ongoing program to support Vermont craftspeople. Silvia Bianchi claimed that Millicent's tweeds actually came from Scotland and the local weavers were in on the deception, but of course you couldn't believe Silvia and anyway, when the full weight of Millicent's presence was upon you, bitchery really didn't fill the bill. What could? Seeing Millicent blown away before your eyes, maybe. Where were the louts who hung around the Northvale gun shop when you really needed them?

"I'm asking for one contribution from each of you. It could be as simple as blueberry muffins or as elaborate as mille-feuille or hazelnut torte, so long as you make it *good.* I know you'll all want to do your best. The higher the bidding, the more money we'll be able to raise. Certainly the cause is good."

Indeed it was. As always. And Amelia, jotting down the particulars along with everybody else, was ashamed of her mental Millicent-baiting. Although Millicent threw her weight around with all the finesse of a bulldozer, none of the thrashing was self-serving. How could you possibly object to being asked to do your bit for the homeless? So you invariably felt guilty about resenting Millicent and her pressure tactics. But resent her everybody did, including survivors of the regime of Edith Van Vliet, wife of the previous president of Northvale, who had turned the campus into a fiefdom.

"Before I let you go, ladies, I want to assure you that we're very close to getting that campus day-care center. There are obstacles, but I intend to surmount them. And I'd like to remind you once again about the counseling service. Whatever the difficulty, someone is there for you, and of course confidentiality is the watchword."

Silence to this last. Everyone remembered how last year Trish Samuels had taken her drinking problem to the counseling service and how the next day the word was all over town. This year Bob Samuels, wifeless, was soldiering on with his push for tenure. Fat chance.

"I shudder to think about that day-care center," Suzanne Longman said to Amelia as they walked out together. " 'Sit down and play with that doll *or else.' "

"Well, at least the kids will be safe. No child molester's going to get past Millicent."

"You're right about that. Still, I'm glad mine are hatched out of the nest and I don't have to think about stuff like that anymore." Suzanne had two grown daughters, one clerking for a law-

4

yer in Philadelphia, the other studying marine biology at Woods Hole. Which you would never guess to look at Suzanne: long, rangy frame without any flab; creamy skin without wrinkles; magnificent mahogany hair without a trace of gray, today swirled into a loose figure eight. Very likely she would be turning heads when she was eighty.

The day was dreary, with a sky the grayest of grays. Earth a mixture of mud and slush. Trees naked and vulnerable. Almost enough to make you wish for more snow. Amelia found her feet dragging as she walked beside Suzanne.

"You're a bundle of laughs today," Suzanne remarked. "What's the matter? Tiff with Gabriel?"

"As a matter of fact, yes. I mean no." Amelia sighed. "He got sore at me yesterday. With good reason. I lost track of the time and was late for Tony LeMaistre's tea."

"Uh-oh." Tony LeMaistre, Northvale College's Shakespeare guru for more than two decades, was given to preparing elaborate dishes that waited for no one. "What was it? The last word in soufflés?" The last last word had featured kumquats and anchovies.

"Guacamole *en croûte.*"

Suzanne laughed, and after a moment Amelia joined in, resolutely pushing aside the memory of Gabriel's ultrapoliteness at breakfast this morning.

They reached Suzanne's bronze Subaru, got in, buckled up. "How far did you get with your sweater?" Suzanne asked as she started the engine.

"All the way up to the neck of the front."

"Good for you."

Amelia leaned back, listening to the engine purr, anticipating a peaceful afternoon. Attending crafts classes was another of Millicent Neumeyer's ideas, intended to benefit local craftspeople and to get faculty wives interacting with the community. Amelia had plumped for knitting over quilting, pottery, weaving, or making little painted animals out of biscuit dough, and, much to her surprise (attempts at knitting in the past had produced disaster), the simple box-weave sweater she was making in a soft olive green wool looked as if it might turn into something she could actually wear. Suzanne, an accomplished knitter, was more or less keeping her company ("because nobody's offering a course in making birchbark canoes").

The knitting classes were held a couple of miles outside town, in the home of Fricka McCardle, a master knitter who had been profiled in numerous crafts publications and president of the Northvale knitters' club, KnitKnacks, to which she donated the class fees. Her house was a trim, blue-accented box, stark amid a bare expanse of brown where, in season, there would be flowers in profusion, along with marrow beans, eggplant, squash, tomatoes, carrots, and a wide variety of herbs. The interior was boxes within a box, and the class met in a parlor that looked as if it had survived intact from a bygone age—maple settee and chairs with patchwork cushions, crystal lamps with pleated shades, a magnificent maple hutch displaying an impressive collection of lusterware. The perfect setting for Fricka, tall and slender and straight as a reed, with soft, barely crumpled camelia-petal skin and an impeccable knot of snowy hair, spotless white blouses and cairngorm brooches. "She's all of a piece," Amelia had once remarked to Suzanne. "I hope I'll be so together when I hit sixty or whatever she is." To which Suzanne had rejoined: "I prefer my period pieces inanimate."

But even Suzanne couldn't fault the way Fricka ran the class, keeping everybody up to the mark and never losing patience. No easy task. There were only seven students, but some days they were clamorous enough for twice that. Suzanne, working on a Kaffe Fassett jacket in soft desert tones, needed only occasional guidance, and the same went for Christine Gotkowski, who had picked up the needles after a long hiatus and was going great guns on a glorious Aran sweater the color of woodbark for her husband Jim, an assistant professor in the math department. Amelia, for her part, had had the sense to choose a project simple enough for a duffer. The other four had not exhibited that kind of sense. To be sure, nothing was simple enough for Anne Wilson, whose swatches of stockinette stitch were so uneven that the idea of a sweater had to be shelved ("for now," Fricka was careful to say); she was making a garter stitch muffler on size seventeen needles, and everybody else was getting lots of practice picking up dropped stitches. Shannon Fiore, working on a seed stitch pull-over, kept losing track of her count and messing up her stitch alignment. Ruth Davidson, a novice at color knitting, had insisted on tackling an elaborate floral pattern and, although the battle with tension was taking its toll on her temper, insisted on perse-vering ("I'll give it to my daughter's anorexic neighbor if it doesn't fit anybody else"). Most troublesome of all was campus glamour girl Elvira Chan, who designed and sewed most of her clothes and, even though she had never knitted before, thought her creativity was threatened by having to follow a pattern. How many times had they all had to listen to Fricka explain—with infi-nite tact—why one of Elvira's "dynamite" ideas wouldn't work?

Today Fricka sorted everybody out with her customary effi-ciency, and soon they were all plugging away, clackety-clackety-clack. The initial topic of conversation was, inevitably, the bake-off. Christine, blonde and aerobics-honed and very compet-itive, was predictably eager to find out what everybody else planned to contribute. Anne said she would make blueberry shortcake "because everybody I've ever served it to goes wild." Ruth, without lifting her head from the yarns she was trying to untangle, said she was thinking about a matzo brei "to gratify somebody with a cast-iron stomach." Amelia and Suzanne said they hadn't decided. Elvira and Shannon said the same, but with the kind of smug smiles that told everybody they were lying. Which drew a huffy "Well, excuse *me*" from Christine. It ended there, without the need of the "Ladies, please!" from Fricka that usually sufficed to quell incipient quarrels.

Talk segued, as so often it did, into the vagaries of Northvale College students. An almost inexhaustible subject. The students, who paid an annual tuition fee that many families throughout the country would have considered themselves blessed to have for an annual income, were spoiled, self-indulgent, self-centered to a de-gree that even the younger faculty members, unabashed repre-sentatives of the me-first/selfishness-is-okay generation, marveled at. Anne knew the real story of why the sign above Northvale Pharmacy, established 1903, had gone missing for a few days: a student had ripped it off (literally) because he thought it would make a super wall hanging for his dormitory room. Elvira, whose next-door neighbor was supervisor of dormitory personnel, told about the junior departing for a winter term at the Sorbonne who couldn't be bothered to pack up her winter clothes—a closetful of Calvin Klein, DKNY, Ralph Lauren, Joan Vass, Perry Ellis—and gave them to the maid. Amelia joined in the general laughter and gave her attention to carrying out Fricka's instructions for shaping the neck of her sweater with unworked and slipped stitches to produce a smooth curve instead of stagger steps.

"What's the big joke?" Ruth said. "They're her clothes. She can do what she wants with them."

Uh-oh. Amelia raised her head quickly. Was this a prelude to one of Ruth's speeches about how frivolity and preoccupation with trivia were women's undoing?

"Personally, I think she could be on the right track." Ruth's Dutch-doll face was coloring up and her brown eyes, round and slightly exophthalmic behind granny glasses, radiated challenge.

Amelia sighed inwardly. Ruth's feminism was a campus byword. It was said that her house was generally a shambles because she insisted on equal division of housework and Sandy Davidson, the shining light of the physics department, was the sort who had difficulty remembering when it was time to eat, let alone when it was his turn to make the bed.

"I doubt if she's on any track at all," Christine said. "I think she's simply a spoiled brat who's had people picking up after her all her life. Like most of the students here."

Ruth smiled sardonically. "And she might think you're a pompous prick. Like most of the faculty and spouses here."

"I think you're way off the mark there, Ruth," Shannon said. "The students at Northvale have a lot of respect for the faculty."

"She's probably got a student snitch with a grudge," Christine said witheringly. "Or maybe she planted a bug in South Dorm." South Dorm was where the more radical element of the student body hung out.

"Come off it, the pair of you. You're too long in the tooth to be conned by the brownnosers and the bootlickers. Everybody knows what most of the students' opinion of the faculty is. What we like to think of as academic dignity translates to them as inflated self-importance."

"Inflated," Suzanne echoed softly. "As in Big-Fish-Little-Pond Syndrome. Stick a pin through the scales—"

"—and the hot air comes rushing out with a lot of hissing and spitting," Ruth said. "And lo and behold, what we have left is an insecure minnow."

"Oh, Lord." Elvira placed a hand over her heart and heaved a melodramatic sigh. "Spare us the pop psychology. Please."

"Amen," said Christine. "Especially the kindergarten variety."

Ruth's face got a little redder. "Well, in present company—"

"That will do, ladies," Fricka said.

"No, it won't!" said Christine. "Why should she have the last word?"

"Stop it now!" Anne said. "I hate all this bickering." She turned on Ruth, and her knitting fell to the floor, the stitches slipping off one of the needles. "Why do you have to focus on the dark side of everything? Northvale is a great place to live, the college is a nice community within a community. What more do you want? Oh, sure, there are things to grumble about, but compared with a lot of other places—well, anyhow, most of us feel pretty secure."

"Except about tenure," Shannon put in. Mike Fiore didn't have it.

"Oh, *that,*" said Anne, with admirable coolness, considering that Barry Wilson was bucking for tenure, too. "Well, sure. But on the whole the atmosphere is pleasant because people have a pretty good understanding of where they're coming from and really, you can't expect much more."

"I can't disagree with that," said Christine, and there were murmurs of assent from Shannon and Elvira.

"I can," Ruth said.

"I have a bit of a problem with it, too," Suzanne said. "Don't you think it might be a tad presumptuous, Anne, speaking for the inner security of a lot of other people? But I guess you're on safe enough ground. There's no way of putting it to the test."

"I wish there were," Ruth said. "Oh, how I wish there were."

"Well, there isn't," said Christine, with a smug little smile, and again there were murmurs of assent from Shannon and Elvira.

They looked, Amelia thought, like three cats with full saucers of pure cream in front of them. All at once she felt an irresistible desire to upend those saucers.

"I wouldn't be too sure of that. How about sending out a bunch of anonymous letters? You know the sort of thing—'You think you have everybody buffaloed, but I know what you've really been up to and so will everybody else before long.' That ought to do it."

Silence.

Stunned silence.

Damn, Amelia thought. Why didn't I keep my big mouth shut? "I was only kidding," she said hastily. "Forget I said it."

"Forget?" Fricka said. *"Forget?* That was just about the most barbarous suggestion I have ever had the misfortune to listen to." Piercing blue eyes bored into Amelia's skull and found the contents beneath contempt.

Amelia's face got hot— That stare was almost enough to make her feel like a child who had just wet the bed. "I said I wasn't serious. Frankly, I found the discussion ridiculous and I thought if I said something still more ridiculous—obviously I didn't think hard enough. I'm sorry."

Fricka's stare did not waver. "Indeed you should be. I find it perfectly appalling that you could suggest sending anonymous letters, even in jest. They would be soul-destroying for anyone, no matter how blameless. I never dreamed you were capable of such cruelty, Amelia."

There was nothing to say to that. Amelia returned her attention to her knitting, wishing the floor would open and swallow her.

"I think you're making too much of it, Fricka," Anne said. "Anonymous letters wouldn't be that big a deal in this day and age. Not if you don't have anything to hide. Most people would probably laugh it off. I know I would."

"*I* wouldn't," Christine said. "I'd be furious. I'd want to wring the neck of my would-be poison pen pal. But I have to agree with Anne that I can't see too many people getting bent out of shape about it."

"Can't you?" Suzanne asked softly.

"Nobody's going to get the chance," Ruth said sharply. "I think we all overreacted to a perfectly innocuous remark because we were all keyed up. And that's my fault. I was way out of line, which isn't that unusual for me, as I'm sure you all know. I'm the one who owes everybody an apology, not Amelia."

"Fair enough," said Christine.

Fricka ventured a small, wan smile. "I'm afraid the biggest overreaction was mine. The idea of anybody poking around in my life simply infuriates me—I place a very high priority on privacy. Naturally, I realize that this makes me something of a dinosaur in an era in which people seem to take pride in putting everything in the front window. Let's say no more about it, shall we?" She held out an imperious hand, palm up. "Let me have that scarf, Anne. You've dropped your stitches. We'd better rescue them before you have hysterics."

Everybody laughed. Or pretended to.

For the rest of the session they all tended to their knitting. The moment Amelia finished shaping the neck of her sweater front, Fricka was at her side to show her how to line up the shoulder stitches of front and back and knit them together. "Next time bring a sixteen-inch circular needle, size six, and we'll work on picking up stitches for the neckband. Many patterns call for leaving that till after the sleeves are sewn in, but I don't hold with that. In the meantime, start working on a sleeve." And she gave Amelia's shoulder a gentle pat, a signal to all that everything was all right.

But Amelia left feeling that everything was far from all right. And it didn't help when, the minute they were buckled into the car, Suzanne said, "That was a dynamite idea of yours, as Elvira would say."

"Don't, Suzanne. Please."

"Lighten up. The way they reacted is their problem, not yours."

"Maybe. But I could kick myself for letting that stupid chatter get to me and losing my cool."

"So what? Proves you're human." Suzanne laughed. "It really was clever. Diabolically clever. Ten to one it's all over town by tomorrow."

Amelia groaned.

"Look at the bright side. You'll be a celebrity. Amelia the scorpion-tongued. If you play your cards right, you'll be able to keep idiots at bay. For a while anyway."

"Go ahead, laugh. Why not? What I mind most is that I truly shocked Fricka."

"So what? She's a dinosaur—she said so herself. Just like her brother, the sainted Siegfried. He used to mount the soapbox at faculty meetings and deplore ad nauseam the fact that politicking had come out of the closet. Maybe she's carrying the privacy torch in his memory. Not that it matters. I doubt if there's anybody in Northvale who doesn't know *her* big secret."

I don't, Amelia thought.

"Anyhow, why should you give a damn about Fricka's good opinion? Nobody else does."

"It's not that. I'm sorry I caused her distress, that's all. If she's managed to preserve her antediluvian attitudes intact, why shake her out of them? And don't bother to tell me about how much the Victorians had to sweep under the rug to maintain those attitudes."

Suzanne laughed. "I'll save my breath, then. No need to worry about what's under Fricka's rug. It's totally harmless."

I'd like to have seen their faces," Gabriel said. "It must have been a hoot."

"I didn't feel like laughing," Amelia said, watching her breath form mist as she jogged in the cold morning air. "Actually, I felt more like crying, out of sheer vexation. I shouldn't have lost control that way."

"You wouldn't be human if you didn't let loose once in a while."

Exactly what Suzanne had said.

"Anyhow, no harm done. Suzanne's your buddy. Ruth may be

a motormouth, but she's not malicious. The others don't really count."

"That's not really the point, is it? I wasn't contemplating the political fallout at the time. Losing it is losing it."

"I know. Just trying to cheer you up." A hesitation. "I guess I lost it with you. Over Tony's tea party."

"I guess you did."

"I shudder to think of the fallout on *that.*"

They both laughed.

Gabriel swerved to his left, put an arm around her waist, gave her a hug, and released her, all without breaking stride.

"Very dexterous."

"No, sinister. It was the left arm."

Amelia groaned.

They jogged on in silence. A very companionable silence. Amelia looked over at Gabriel, running easily at her side. After more than a decade of marriage, he still stirred her senses as profoundly as ever. Sometimes she thought there was something indecent in that. But what the hell, the man was gorgeous. Six feet tall in the cowboy boots he habitually wore, slim and wiry, he had, in the past, bemoaned a lack of beefcake; the era of Nordic Track and lean cuisine put him right in style. The burgundy sweats she had given him for his birthday set off his black hair and olive skin and vibrant green eyes to perfection. She could take no credit for his features, which had the clarity and symmetry of a Donatello sculpture, though he believed they lacked distinction and periodically threatened to grow a beard. Amelia didn't care for the idea, but who knew? A beard might make him more gorgeous yet.

"Time to head home," Gabriel said. "You're starting to huff and puff like the Little Engine That Couldn't."

"I am not."

"Well, I am." He turned and started back to the house.

Amelia smiled as she followed suit, knowing that Gabriel could go a good few miles more without breathing hard. An enthusiastic jogger, he got in his mileage most mornings at the track in the college gym because the ground was often too squishy or too snowy to make outdoor jogging feasible. Amelia had never developed the jogger's mind-set, having been turned off when they lived in New York by the hordes of joggers with Walkmans in their ears and fanaticism in their eyes; she kept herself fit with a stretching/toning regime she had obtained back in her college days from one of her physical education instructors, a former dancer with the Joffrey Ballet. However, when she had the chance to jog beside Gabriel on a tree-lined road they had to themselves, she enjoyed it.

Especially on mornings like this, sunny and crisp with a portent of frost in the air. She had awakened to a house redolent of coffee, which Gabriel had made. He had also prepared breakfast. Supportiveness. Just what she needed. Yesterday, when she had told him about knitting class, he had been quick to tell her not to worry about it. This morning he was going out of his way to reinforce the message. Which made her feel terrific.

All at once Gabriel stopped short. Straight ahead, at the side of the road, stood a child bundled up in gum boots and baggy pants, a red-and-black plaid jacket and a too-big cap with the earflaps down. Boy? Girl? Impossible to tell. The child was motionless, staring at them blankly.

Amelia stopped, too. "Are you lost?"

The words had a galvanizing effect. The child turned and started running through the trees and soon disappeared from view.

They resumed jogging home. Amelia felt let down, as if the harmony she had been tuned to had sounded a sour note.

2

The woman with the bush of gray hair wore a dark blue down coat and had her arms wrapped around a big brown shopping bag. Her face was a blur as Amelia drove past, but something about the profile and the Colette-like mane stirred recognition. She slowed down and studied the rearview mirror. The woman was Katherine Ellsworth, wife of the chairman of the Northvale English department.

Amelia stopped her VW Rabbit and waited, engine idling, till Katherine came abreast. "Hello, Katherine. Can I give you a lift?"

Katherine's square, weather-beaten face brightened, dimmed in a flash. "It's pretty far out of your way, I'm afraid. Anyway, I could do with the exercise."

"You've obviously walked from the market. That's exercise enough for anybody." Amelia leaned over and opened the passenger door. "Hop in."

Katherine smiled and got into the car, bringing with her a pungent odor of earth and sweat. "Mine's in the garage. Transmission. Thank you."

Two miles at least from her house to the nearest market, Amelia calculated, and the return trip would seem twice as long with that bag of groceries. "It's a good thing I happened to be passing by."

"Yes. On your way back from Rutland?"

Amelia hesitated. "Sort of." Actually, she had been to the home of a marine archaeologist to confer about editing his memoirs, should he ever manage to stay out of the water and sober long enough to get them on tape. But what business was it of Katherine's?

"Sorry. I was making conversation, not prying." A sigh. "I seem to be losing all my social graces in my old age."

Amelia was instantly contrite. "No apology necessary. I guess I sounded a little testy."

"Can't say I blame you. Living in Northvale must be like living in a goldfish bowl for you."

"Somewhat. I should be used to it by now, though."

"Why? You're not a goldfish, are you?"

Amelia laughed, and Katherine joined in with a dry, raspy chuckle that sounded as if it had been in mothballs for a while.

"I wasn't really looking forward to the trek home," Katherine admitted. "Kind of you to stop for me."

"Not at all." Amelia had "Anyone would have done the same" on the tip of her tongue and checked it. Anyone wouldn't, apparently. Not in Vermont. She remembered Steve Dubofsky of the sociology department telling her about the class assignment he had given to find out whether Vermonters were really as callous as they were cracked up to be. One student had pulled his car over to the side of the road, lifted the hood, and mimed misery; in the space of an hour, forty-three cars had whizzed by and two had stopped to offer assistance, one from New Jersey and one from Ontario.

"It's the next turnoff on the right."

"I know." Amelia had visited the Ellsworth house years ago, as part of the obligatory round of tea-party hospitality the Northvale English department offered its new members ("Running the gauntlet," Gabriel had called it); the occasion had lingered in her mind because of the glorious, dazzling late summer blossoms enveloping the house like some lavish outdoor set for the entr'acte of *The Sleeping Beauty,* and she had made it a point to drive past the house in spring and summer to look at the flowers.

The house was no castle, merely a smallish two-story box with white siding that could have done with a coat of paint, and now, surrounded by slush, it looked rather bleak. "You have a good memory," Katherine remarked, as Amelia drove up to the side door. On impulse, Amelia confessed that the garden fascinated her and that she often drove past to see it. "I've never seen anything like it. It's so untrammeled, almost as if everything's growing wild. I suppose that sounds like disparaging all your hard work, but I didn't mean it to."

Katherine gave her rusty-sounding laugh. "It sounds about right, only most people wouldn't say it. They're brought up to think of gardens as nice, tidy places. Bluebells here, marigolds there. I was, and I never even imagined there might be another way until I went to Jamaica and happened to wander off the beaten track and came upon this garden that was almost jungle— you had to slither between the plants. Barbaric, a bit frightening, and absolutely the most beautiful thing I'd ever seen. The gardener was an old Maroon woman, and when I asked her how she did it she said the seeds spoke to her, told her where they wanted to go. I've never forgotten that and—" The laugh again, slightly embarrassed. "Well, of course the messages don't come in as loud and clear for me as they did for her."

Amelia said they seemed to come in loud and clear enough, which elicited an invitation to come and see the garden anytime she chose. Her "I'd love to" was just a shade too enthusiastic and trapped her into fielding, "Do you have time for a cup of coffee?" She would have liked to beg off on the grounds that she had a full day ahead of her (perfectly true), but a flash of what looked like appeal in the older woman's eyes stopped her.

The little storeroom inside the door had the old country house smell of mildew and bad drainage, but in the kitchen all Amelia could smell was coffee, brewed to the burning point. The kitchen had been fitted out in the days when nobody thought of any color but white for appliances, and it was clean and attractive enough, with a lot of delft blue on display—tiles, curtains, enamel pots, crockery, glassware—but it left Amelia, who wasn't big on blue and white, cold.

Katherine opened the refrigerator and stuffed the whole bag of groceries inside. "Can't be bothered to unpack now. I think we'll have our coffee in the dining room. How does that sound?"

"Like an awful lot of trouble."

"Not a bit of it. The coffee's already made, as a matter of fact. All I have to do is pour it. Aren't these modern coffeemakers that brew up a whole day's supply wonderful?"

"Wonderful," Amelia agreed, barely able to repress a shudder at what her nose was telling her about that coffee. She followed Katherine out of the kitchen and across the hall into the dining room. Here, too, blue and white dominated—a wealth of porcelain, resting on shelves and in niches that appeared to have been specially constructed, as in museums. There was even a glass case under the window, holding a two-foot-high porcelain cylinder decorated with a landscape depicting houses with pagoda roofs, trees, and a river with a bridge over it and a sailboat in it.

"It's an umbrella stand," Katherine said. "They're very rare. This one belonged to my grandmother. I couldn't possibly afford to buy it. Especially nowadays—prices have hit the sky. Do you know anything about Canton ware?"

"Not a thing. Some of it is quite lovely." The compliment sounded lukewarm. Amelia regretted not having faked more enthusiasm.

Katherine grinned. "You must be a stoneware person. Rough, primitive shapes. Earth colors. Am I right?"

"I'm afraid so. But I like porcelain, too."

"Sure. When it's not being too uppity." The grin widened. "I'll get the coffee."

Left alone, Amelia took a tour of the room, which, formal as it was, generated a warmth that the kitchen lacked. Her attention was caught by a mahogany block-front kneehole desk with three shells carved on the top drawer, the two on the sides raised and the one in the center recessed, as was another shell carved inside the kneehole. She recalled having seen a similar piece at the Metropolitan Museum of Art.

"Something else I inherited from Gran," Katherine said as

18

she came in and set a brass tray holding two large white china mugs, sugar bowl, and creamer on the dining table, a massive oak affair with claw feet. "We're using ordinary crockery, not the Canton. I hope you won't take it as an insult."

"God, no. After what you just told me, I'd be afraid to touch any of it." Amelia sat down at the table and accepted a mug, declining cream and sugar. "Just how valuable is it, anyway?"

"Hard to give figures, even ballpark—they seem to rise every day. The fascinating thing about the boom is that initially export porcelain was a relatively unimportant part of the China trade. Tea and silks were the hot ticket items, and the crates of china served more or less as ballast—paving the ship, they called it. Cooks often threw dirty plates overboard because china was plentiful and clean water wasn't. Later, of course, it became immensely popular in the West, and eventually collectors cornered the market. For a long time Canton lagged behind famille rose and rose medallion and the more elaborate stuff, but lately it's been catching up. A pity, really. It's unpretentious stuff. I like that. I also like the fact that it's blue and white—real kitchen colors."

Amelia smiled noncommittally and took a sip of coffee. Too big a sip—thick and strong and bitter, the coffee seemed to corrode her throat.

"I guess this lot ranks as a minicollection," Katherine said. "Most of it comes from Gran, who had a real eye for the unusual. What she left goes way beyond the usual company dinnerware that's come down through a lot of New England families. Other things I picked up here and there, when you could buy the odd piece without filing for bankruptcy. A little bowl like that"—she gestured at a bowl about four inches in diameter—"is going for three hundred dollars."

"Oh, my." Amelia was taken aback. "What would something like that octagonal ginger jar be worth?"

"Tea caddy. Ginger jars are shorter and wider. Thousands, I expect. That was Gran's, too." Katherine sighed. "I once saw one of those that still had the original lid, which is almost unheard of. I dreamed about it for weeks."

"Weeks when you could hardly wait for sack time, I'll bet."

"You might put it that way." Katherine chuckled. "I've been told that you could turn a phrase inside out. I understand that your most recent sally has been a nine-days wonder."

Amelia groaned. "Don't remind me. It feels more like ninety."

"That's Northvale for you. In New York you wouldn't rate nine minutes."

"Right on," Amelia said, with more fervor than she intended.

Katherine laughed heartily, and Amelia joined in, thinking, with some surprise, that there was more to Katherine Ellsworth than the dour, dowdy eccentric of campus legend, and not much liking herself for the surprise.

"Hang on a minute." Katherine sprang out of her chair. "There's something I want to show you." She dashed out of the room.

While Katherine's chukkas thumped up the stairs, Amelia worked at getting down a polite amount of coffee. No small task—it was like swallowing charred mud.

Katherine came back carrying a slender, tapering Canton candlestick with a hand-dipped candle in it. "I keep this on my nightstand. The candle's just for show—I'd never light it. There aren't many Canton candlesticks about. I bought this about twenty years ago from a very old lady who could have sold it for three or four times what I was able to pay her, but she could see how much I wanted it."

"The shape is lovely."

"Isn't it?" Katherine sat down and set the candlestick gently on the table and reached for Amelia's hand. "Feel the texture."

"It's so grainy. Almost like pigskin. How odd—it looks so smooth."

"The older pieces are always like that. And very, very heavy." Katherine reached into the pocket of her slacks and pulled out a very small shallow bowl. "This is an open salt. Rare as can be these days. The moment I set eyes on it I knew I just had to have it. Isn't it exquisite beyond belief? Take a close look at the design."

Amelia looked, and saw the by now familiar house with pagoda roof, the tree, the river, the bridge, the boat. She produced what she hoped was a rapturous murmur and glanced at Katherine's face to see if she'd brought it off.

And got a shock. Katherine was staring at the little salt with an intensity that was almost frightening. In that stare was admiration, longing, and something Amelia couldn't quite read. Shame? Guilt? She averted her eyes quickly, conscious that she had seen more than she should have seen. Clearly Katherine Ellsworth had invested a lot of emotional as well as financial capital in her Canton. Too much. Far too much.

Amelia forced down a few more swallows of coffee. Who was she to make that judgment? Anyway, it was none of her business. She glanced at Katherine again and saw, with relief, a gaze focused inward now. She set her mug down on the brass tray and pushed back her chair. "Well, that made a nice break. I'll be on my way now. Thank you."

Katherine roused herself to a perfunctory politeness and repeated her invitation to visit the garden "whenever you like. I'll be happy to give you cuttings of anything you fancy." But the warmth she had exuded only minutes ago was gone. It was almost as if her visitor had ceased to exist for her.

Amelia drove home slightly nettled at the summary sendoff, and wondering about it. With someone else, she might have taken it for recollection of rank, a "What am I doing baring my soul to the wife of a lowly assistant professor?" But with Katherine Ellsworth, it had to be something else.

Never mind what else. Amelia preferred not to think about it, and regretted not having taken another route home.

3

When it came to cuisine, Amelia had always practiced what she had read somewhere was Mike Schmidt's theory on batting: KISS, or Keep It Simple, Stupid. If it worked for Mike Schmidt, why shouldn't it work for her? It should. It did—until she came to Northvale and discovered that inviting guests to dinner, to hear many of the faculty wives tell it, meant preparing Peking duck, a cassoulet, a fifty-dish ristafel or curry. Shaken, she enrolled in gourmet cooking classes at the Well-Tempered Cleaver, where the proprietress, Terry Tracy, savvy enough to know that there isn't a Julia Child in everyone, convinced her that there was nothing wrong with the KISS theory; that you could send a score of people home happy after a meal of pasta and salad, if you made the sauce for the pasta good enough and chose the freshest possible vegetables for the salad. Thanks to Terry, Amelia was able to face up to entertaining without feeling she was entering a competition, and the results had not disgraced her or Gabriel—the bottom line, after all.

The bake-off *was* a competition, no way round that. The mere thought of trying to turn out something to stand beside the sure-to-be-spectacular tortes, layer cakes, shortcakes, flans, pies, strudels, and whatnot was daunting, so Amelia tried to think about it as little as possible till the time came to deliver. Because her offering was going to be very humble: gingerbread. Terrific gingerbread, to be sure. She had taken off from a James Beard recipe that included sour cream, zinged up the cinnamon and ginger, added a dash of dark rum to the butter/molasses mixture, and invented a honey/cream frosting studded with crystallized ginger.

The morning of baking day found her at Pure Priorities, the natural foods co-op, assembling her ingredients. The co-op was busy, and she spotted a number of faculty wives, no doubt doing what she was doing. As she approached the spice section, she almost collided with a cart propelled by redheaded, freckle-faced Arlene de Jong, whose husband taught computer science. Arlene murmured, "Sorry," her face turned the color of her hair, and she hurried away, dragging her redheaded, freckle-faced little boy after her. "Fee-fi-fo-fum," Amelia muttered under her breath, noting that the contents of Arlene's cart added up to chocolate cake.

The big jar of crystallized ginger was almost full. Amelia spooned far more than she needed into a plastic bag (a bit of self-indulgence with leftovers wouldn't hurt), closed the jar and replaced it on the shelf, reached for the jar of powdered ginger.

"Hello, little gray wren," said a voice beyond her. "Little" was ever so slightly "leetle." Silvia Bianchi. "You will note that I greet you as a friend so you will not poison your pen on me." A peal of laughter, loud and resounding like a carillon.

Amelia turned around, forcing herself to smile at the tall, lean woman with the improbably black hair who confronted her. Just as Enrico Bianchi presided over the Northvale College Italian department, his wife presided over the Northvale College gossip mill.

"Hello, Silvia. You don't have to worry, I do all my correspondence at the typewriter these days. My God, you'd think everybody would be sick of the whole thing by now."

"Oh no, *cara*. This is a small town. One grows tired of talking about who is running around with whom and who is running out of time at the bank. Only the names change, not the news. You have made a truly original contribution."

"I wish I'd bitten my tongue instead."

"That would have been a very great pity." Another peal of laughter, a wave of the hand, and Silvia was gone.

Amelia didn't dally packaging up the powdered ginger, some powdered cloves, some powdered cinnamon; nor in getting butter and sour cream and sweet cream from the dairy section. She kept her head down to avoid eye contact with anyone, and she managed to get out of the co-op without having to engage in further conversation.

Going home felt like fleeing to sanctuary. She told herself she was making too much of the whole thing, but since when did knowing you were behaving like an idiot act as a deterrent? The house had never seemed more welcoming. Architecturally, it was no great shakes, just the typical New England box house, three rooms upstairs and three down. But it had been the best thing going, because of a hilltop location and the view that went with it, enhanced by the big picture window installed by the previous owner, a free spirit of nomadic bent, who had also knocked down the walls downstairs for an open living space (Amelia longed to do the same upstairs and install a skylight, but of course Gabriel needed an office and a door he could shut), not to mention the astonishingly low price.

The most striking feature of the downstairs living space, Amelia often thought, was that sometimes, depending on the mood you were in, the kitchen area, with its brick walls, floor of terracotta tiles, semicircular teak counter jutting outward, its panoply of copper and brass and iron and pottery suspended from a ceiling carousel, seemed to take the place over, and the ambience was warm and picturesque domesticity (unearned, but what the hell). A different story when her workplace, another semicircular teak counter, was in operation, but today typewriter, books, manuscripts, paper, and the rest of her paraphernalia were shelved underneath the counter and there was only the stoneware pencil jar on the surface.

She got to work immediately, resolving, as she set the oven at 350 degrees, that this would be the best gingerbread she had ever made. Certainly a cut above Arlene de Jong's chocolate cake, which would probably derive from *Gourmet* or the *Time/Life* Good Cook series.

Cheap shot. So Arlene had snubbed her. So what? Why should she care?

She shouldn't, but she did. The only comfort was that her newfound notoriety couldn't last much longer. Still, in the meantime it was a royal pain in the ass.

She set the pan with butter and molasses over a moderate flame, stirred gently until the mixture came to a boil, turned off the flame and set the pan aside to cool. While she was sifting the stone-ground flour, the phone rang.

It was Gabriel. "You're probably going to want to shoot me for this, but I invited a guest to tea this afternoon."

Amelia laughed. "Why should I want to shoot you? It's your house."

"It's also criminally short notice. But I was talking to William and happened to mention that we finally got around to making slides of the photographs we took during the Pilgrimage and one thing led to another and before I knew it—"

"Say no more. I wish I could offer crumpets and homemade marmalade, but alas . . ."

Gabriel laughed. "I thought cinnamon toast? With the orange pekoe my sister sent? Is that okay?"

"Sure. It's no trouble at all. And even if it were, I wouldn't mind. He's a nice man." Perfectly true. William Ellsworth, head of the Northvale English department, ran a fairly taut ship without arousing ill will in underlings—no mean feat. Moreover, his classes in early-nineteenth-century poetry and prose (major-league turnoffs on other campuses) were extremely popular with students, although they involved a huge amount of reading and he was by no means an easy grader.

"Four-ish." Pause. "I'm lucky to have you."

"Flattery will get you anywhere you want to go."

The minute she hung up, Amelia checked the freezer, found the better part of a loaf of wholemeal bread. She took it out. Sliced, spread with butter and honey and a lot of cinnamon, popped under the broiler for a minute or two—short-order ambrosia. She dusted, fluffed pillows, went over the parquet and the tiles with a dust mop. William Ellsworth would have nothing to complain of on any front.

The butter/molasses mixture was sufficiently cool by now. She added a generous splash of rum, folded in sour cream. She sifted in the flour and the spices, stirring until the batter was smooth and creamy, then poured it into a buttered earthenware cake pan and put the pan in the oven and set the timer for forty minutes.

There was time, she decided, to get in a little work on the manuscript she was currently editing. She settled herself into the Windsor chair behind her work counter and pulled out the box holding the unbound pages and set it out. And sighed. Many of the manuscripts she worked on had limited appeal, and this one, as far as she could see, had none at all. Who wanted to read the memoirs of a bartender at the watering hole frequented by Ronald Reagan during the late forties and early fifties? But some editor thought there was a market: money had been paid to the author and money would be paid to her.

The timer pinged as she was tightening a speech on the hazards of stardom attributed to Ronald Reagan but improbably fatuous even for him. She put the manuscript away and went to take the gingerbread out of the oven. The smell, faint until she opened the oven door, suddenly filled the kitchen. The gingerbread looked as good as it smelled. She chopped some of the crystallized ginger and set it aside. She softened butter with a wooden spoon, added honey to produce a thick golden goo, folded in cream to thin the texture and pale the gold, folded in the chopped ginger.

Time to get herself ready. She went upstairs and, as she splashed water on her face, took a critical look at herself in the mirror above the sink. Her hair didn't need attention. Originally auburn, it had started to turn gray when she was seventeen, and ten years later she decided to give up the battle and go with it, over a lot of protests, including Gabriel's. Happily, the gray was silvery, and opting to go with the natural curl in a short, tousled mop gave her a certain cachet. Even Gabriel had learned to like it (one moon-drenched night, running his fingers through it, he had commented, "I guess it's not every man who gets to bang a wraith on a regular basis," and gone on to prove he enjoyed the experience). To make up or not to make up? Not, she decided. Her color was as good as naturally pale skin ever gets, and enhancing her almost black eyes in the daytime was overkill. A touch of lip gloss would do it.

What to wear? She plumped for a favorite standby, an oversize silk black-and-white tweed top, which could be dressed up with a skirt or down with pants. Down was the order of the day, so it would be her black cords.

The gingerbread was frosted and she was drizzling honey over thick slices of buttered wholemeal bread when she heard the purr of the new Volvo, bought last summer to celebrate getting tenure.

Gabriel came in and darted up the stairs like a whirlwind. "I'm late, damn it. Wet student conference. Buckets of tears over a C-plus grade. Can you believe it?"

"Were they genuine?"

"God knows. It was an exam, not a paper, so all I could do was tell her to work harder and shove Kleenex at her—she went through half a box." A furious clattering overhead. A cry of joy. "Everything's exactly where it should be, thank God. When William gets here, send him straight up, will you?"

"Sure. I presume you'll want a tray?"

"I guess so. If it's not too much trouble."

"No trouble. Could you get the serving table?"

"Right." Gabriel dashed down the stairs to the front closet, collected the walnut folding table, blew a kiss, and dashed back up the stairs.

Amelia smiled as she recapped the honey jar. She turned on the oven, got out the cinnamon, and sprinkled it with a lavish hand.

William Ellsworth was punctual, as Amelia knew he would be. Her crumpets-and-marmalade crack earlier had been a little unfair, implying stuffiness, and he wasn't stuffy, he just looked as if he should be. Tall and spare, addicted to hacking jackets, suede elbow patches, and briar pipes, with hair like polished silver and skin like creased parchment, he was almost a walking magazine illustration of an English country squire. Incongruous to think of him mated with Katherine: Lord Peter Wimsey and Raggedy Ann.

Cruel and doubtless unfair. Appearances weren't everything, weren't even very much.

Still, Lord Peter wasn't a bad analogy. William Ellsworth's

manner, assuring Amelia that she was doing him the greatest kindness in having him for tea, was positively courtly. And then he took a deep sniff, and the courtier turned into a little boy. "Is that fresh gingerbread I smell?"

"Yes. I baked it for—"

"I knew it." A rapturous smile that illuminated his clear hazel eyes like a beam of sunlight. "How marvelous. Do you know, I can't recall the last time anyone baked gingerbread for me. Thank you."

Amelia forced herself to smile back. "Don't rejoice too soon. The taste might not live up to the smell."

He laughed at this and went upstairs to join Gabriel. With a sigh, Amelia set to work making tea. Good-bye to all her hard work. Now she would have to dash out for more sour cream, more sweet cream, more butter, more everything, the whole tedious gingerbread routine to do all over again.

It didn't help that, when she took up the tea tray, both Gabriel and William Ellsworth expressed disappointment when she begged off the slide show because she had errands to run. Their disappointment was politeness. Hers was real. After a hard day at the oven, she would have liked nothing better than to relive the Pilgrimage.

For it had truly been a pilgrimage. A tour of British literary shrines, undertaken during the year spent abroad to do research for Gabriel's dissertation on Dante Gabriel Rossetti. Before they left, they had marked a map of the British Isles with scores of red dots, and, while it wouldn't be entirely accurate to say they hadn't missed one, they hadn't missed many. Stratford on Avon and Dublin, the Lakes District and the moors of Haworth, the Scilly Isles and the Aran Islands and the Hebrides—they had covered a lot of turf when they weren't beavering away under the great dome of the British Museum. Not to mention the pavements of London. Drury Lane. The Cheshire Cheese, haunt of Dr. Johnson. The Keats House in Hampstead. The Church of St. Mary-le-bone, where Robert Browning and Elizabeth Barrett had tied the knot. And, of course, 16 Cheyne Walk, Rossetti's home, famous in its day for its chinoiserie, its menagerie, and its floating, not always compatible human population (to George Meredith was attributed a desire to kick Algernon Swinburne down the stairs if it weren't for the noise his horrid little bottom would make bouncing from step to step). Yes, they had seen just about everything they wanted to see, and they had the pictures to keep the memories fresh. Amelia wondered which ones Gabriel had chosen to show to William Ellsworth. Maybe, she thought as she closed the curtains against the coming of dark, she could make it back for the tail end.

It wasn't to be. At Pure Priorities she ran into Pam Blair, an instructor in the English department, who looked as if the sky had fallen on her head. There was nothing for it but to stop for coffee and listen. It was bad. Pam had been at Northvale for three years and had made a fine thing of the black literature course she was pioneering. But the year was far advanced and she had heard nothing about a contract for next year. "I may be female and black, but I can easily be replaced by a black lesbian—tokenism on three fronts instead of two." A statement Amelia, knowing departmental politics as she did, could not refute. Nor could she, knowing the tightness of the job market, offer any words of comfort. All she could do was promise to find out from Gabriel what, if anything, he knew about it and pass the word on to Pam. This earned her a wry smile. "I'd appreciate it. And thanks for sparing me the Pollyanna bullshit. I'll tell you frankly, Amelia, the way I feel about this place now—Well, don't be surprised if I plant a bomb on campus before I'm out of here."

William Ellsworth was gone when Amelia got home, and Gabriel was ensconced in the black leather armchair, dozing, a copy of *Possession* on the floor alongside. She smiled and, despite the weight of the bag of groceries in her arms (the co-op had taken in a shipment of wonderful grapefruit and oranges since this morning), stopped beside the chair and bent down to brush his forehead with her lips. He didn't wake.

She went to put the groceries away. The tea tray was on the drainboard of the sink. The dirty dishes were in the dishwasher, and she checked them to be sure they'd been scraped. There was no trace of gingerbread anywhere. She wondered what had become of it. Surely there had been too much for two people to put away? Well, maybe they had skipped lunch.

Better, she decided, to forego the boeuf Bourguignon she had taken out of the freezer this morning—much too heavy for a stomach full of gingerbread. An omelet and a green salad, with fruit and cheese and perhaps that cinnamon toast (or would that be better for breakfast?). Right after dinner she would bake more gingerbread. Which meant double duty with Ronald Reagan's bartender tomorrow.

She was at the sink shredding romaine lettuce when Gabriel tiptoed up behind her and circled her waist with his arms. "That was sensational gingerbread," he murmured in her ear.

"It must have been, the way you pigged out."

"I only had one slice. William had three, and I gave him the rest to take home. I knew you wouldn't mind."

"Of course not. Anyway, the damage was already done. It was supposed to be my contribution to the bake-off for the homeless."

"Aw, shit. Why didn't you tell him?"

"I didn't have the heart. The minute he set foot in the door he started sniffing like a hungry hound and telling me how great it was that somebody baked gingerbread just for him. How could I deny him?"

"Nobody ever can. The wings off birds, as they say, and anything else the birds might have to—Never mind. He said it was the best gingerbread he's ever tasted, if that does anything for you."

"Not much."

"Bummer." He gave her waist a squeeze. "Tell you what. Forget about cooking dinner. We'll go out. That new Italian place. Angel hair with pesto and veal piccata. How does that sound?"

"Heavenly. But—"

"Don't argue. Just go up and put on a skirt and the pagodas while I fix us both a long, tall wine cooler."

"You talked me into it." She dropped the romaine into the colander to deal with later. Going up the stairs, she suddenly felt a craving for a short, squat martini, extra dry (whisper "vermouth" into the glass), hesitated, and continued on up. Not fair to indulge when Gabriel couldn't—he had to drive.

It took no time at all to change from the black cords to a long black flannel skirt and put on the earrings Gabriel was so fond of, delicate pagoda-shaped drops of silver filigree they had picked up on the Portobello Road. She ran a comb through her hair, collected her black leather pouch, and came down to a transformed house. Gabriel had turned off the lights and opened the curtains to a moonlit night sky, the Green Mountains looming high and remote against a backdrop of midnight blue streaked with purple—a vista so otherworldly you almost expected to see the Queen of the Night appear. Amelia sat down on the sofa beside Gabriel and took the glass he held out to her. As promised, long and tall and cold. Who needed a martini? She felt that there was nowhere on the planet she would rather be than in gloriously beautiful Vermont with Gabriel beside her.

But the memory of Pam Blair's unhappy face nagged at her: she had, after all, given a promise. "I ran into Pam Blair this afternoon," she said casually. "She's worried that her contract isn't going to be renewed." She paused, but Gabriel didn't jump in. "I was wondering if you'd heard anything about it."

He took a deliberate sip of his drink. Then, with a sigh, "She's right, I'm afraid."

"Oh, Gabriel, what a shame. She's such a good teacher."

"You know as well as I do that's seldom where it's at. The problem is, she's too militant for some of—"

"For God's sake, she's hardly Angela Davis!"

"Well, she can be a bit abrasive and—"

"—and the fossilized powers that be prefer a voice 'soft, gentle, and low—an excellent thing in woman,' and sexism triumphs again. What a crock! I'll bet Sam Rigby is raising the roof."

Gabriel hesitated. "He didn't support her."

"What?" Amelia was stunned. Samson Rigby was black and a full professor; he had campaigned hard for another African American in the department and Pam had been his choice. "Why on earth not?"

"I'm not sure, but—" Another hesitation. "I think it has to do with that black lit course. I suspect he wants to teach it himself."

"Oh my God. Are you telling me he let her devise it and launch it as a trial balloon for himself?"

"No, no, it's nowhere near as bad as that. He's unhappy with the slant she's given it. He was up in arms when he looked at her syllabus and saw she'd scheduled half a lecture on Ralph Ellison and a whole one on Alice Walker. At the risk of sounding sexist myself, I have to say I think Ellison's worth more attention than Walker."

"That's not really the point, is it? If it's her course—"

"Yeah, well, that should be the bottom line, but it never is."

"I suppose not." Her opinion of Sam Rigby, a big, bearlike man with a deep, mellow voice and a hearty laugh, who never paraded his big reputation in his field (twentieth-century American literature), went down several notches. She recalled Pam's referring to him once as "our poor man's James Earl Jones" and quickly asking Amelia to "forget I ever said that. I wouldn't want it to get back to him. I've seen him in his Darth Vader mode and once was enough."

"I have to admit I'll be sorry to see Pam go," Gabriel said. "She livened up faculty meetings no end."

"She thinks she'll probably be replaced by a black lesbian. But I suppose it's as likely to be a gay Hispanic."

"Close. He's Chinese. Sexual persuasion undisclosed, but he's a protegé of Eliot Parking."

Amelia groaned.

Gabriel slid his arm around her and kissed her temple lightly. "I know. All the departmental politicking can be a real drag, but what can you do?" He kissed her again, a little more vigorously. "You look good enough to eat. Which reminds me. Drink up and let's go let the world have a look at the flavor of the month, celebrity of the moment, or what you will."

"Ouch." Amelia forced herself to laugh. "I hate it that a silly, thoughtless remark like mine circulates like a brush fire. Everybody I've run into lately has heard it—I can tell." Recalling Arlene de Jong's reaction, Amelia took a deep swallow from her glass. "Not that they say anything about it. Except Silvia Bianchi. Fortunately, she was amused."

"Well, of course she was. Anybody with any sense would be amused. Most of the people who mentioned it to me said they're waiting to see what you do for an encore."

"They'll have a long wait. From now on I think twice before I open my mouth. Maybe three times."

"Life in the slow lane? Sounds boring." He tilted her face toward his and kissed her lips. "I have a little surprise for you. I was going to spring it over dinner, but what the hell. Steve called me last week. He'll be off on a dig for a couple of months and offered us the use of the apartment. So we can treat ourselves to a trip to New York over the winter recess. A little miracle, isn't it?"

"God, yes." Steve was an archaeologist, possessor of a rent-controlled apartment, which Gabriel had been sharing when she had met him and fallen madly in love with him and found out her feeling was returned. Halcyon days. Passionate nights. She could feel her spirits take wing.

"Just think. Back in the bed where we made love for the first time."

That brought her back down. Fast. "Umm," she murmured.

He kissed her again. "I'll bring the car out front."

Amelia sat motionless when he was gone. Remembering. They had made love innumerable times in Steve's apartment, but the first time had been in the little white Fiat Gabriel drove back then. She had protested that there wasn't room, he had said there was and proved it; later, he had admitted resorting to surprise tactics because she had seemed so stiff and skittish. She felt an unfamiliar pang, thinking back. He should have remembered.

So he didn't remember. So what? Men weren't as sentimental as women, that was all.

The horn honked. Amelia sprang to her feet, turned on the lamp on the table beside the sofa, closed the curtains against the night. She would, she decided, go for that martini at the restaurant. Or at least a gin and tonic.

4

YOU THINK NOBODY KNOWS WHAT YOU'VE BEEN UP TO BUT YOU'RE WRONG. I KNOW. PRETTY SOON EVERYBODY WILL KNOW. NOTHING YOU CAN DO ABOUT IT EXCEPT REPENT.

"Oh my God." Amelia dropped the letter and covered her face with her hands. "Oh my *God.*"

"What is it?" Gabriel pushed back his chair and came around the table behind her and picked up the letter. "Jesus."

Amelia began to shudder. She took her hands down from her face and hugged her arms. Tight. Tighter.

"It's a joke, Amelia. A nasty, disgusting practical joke. Has to be."

"Probably, but that doesn't make it any easier to take. I really pissed somebody off, didn't I?"

"It would seem so." Gabriel picked up the envelope. "Word processor or computer. Naturally. Once upon a time they could ID a typewriter to pinpoint the perp, but technology has done wonders to protect the anonymity of criminals."

"I wish I could be anonymous, too. God, how I wish I'd kept my big mouth shut."

"So do I. For your peace of mind, not because I think you said anything that terrible. Look at the up side, Amelia. Somebody wanted to send you a message and did. Period." He picked up her fork and put it in her hand. "You said you were hungry enough to eat a horse."

"That was then. This is now." But she went to work on the spinach frittata. Cold, of course, but tasty enough, if she could somehow manage to revive her appetite.

They had been on the road since late afternoon, deciding not to stop for dinner. Once home, Amelia had busied herself in the kitchen straightaway, while Gabriel hung up coats, took suitcases upstairs, sorted mail. She had not even glanced at her letters until the food was on the table, and it was her habit to open her mail in increasing order of interest, so the white envelope with no return address, which she had expected to contain a flyer for a new thrift shop or auto parts outlet, got immediate attention.

A joke, Gabriel said. Probably he was right. Not a bit funny, but nobody ever said practical jokes had to be funny, except to the joker.

Maybe it wasn't meant to be funny at all. Maybe somebody had been as offended by her witless witticism as Fricka McCardle had been and wanted to give her a taste of her own medicine. Likely. Very likely.

She wondered what she should do about it. Ignore it? Spread the word that she had got the message and beat her breast a little to advertise repentance? Would that appease the letter writer?

Why the hell should she want to appease the letter writer?

A car pulled up outside. A car door slammed. Slow, heavy footsteps approached the house.

Amelia shuddered and hugged herself again. "Ta-ta-ta-ta," she murmured. "Just like the end of *Don Giovanni*. He wouldn't repent either, and look what happened to him."

Gabriel scowled. "Knock it off, Amelia."

"Sorry. Rotten joke." But it really hadn't been a joke. Not when those footsteps had such a graveyard resonance.

The doorbell chimed and Gabriel went to answer it. Let in not the marble statue of the Commendatore but a reasonable facsimile—uniformed and booted patrolman Tom Tracy. Amelia's disquietude increased a hundredfold. Tracy, gangly and sandy-haired and freckle-faced, Tom Sawyer grown to manhood, looked uneasy. Or was he merely embarrassed at paying an official visit to someone who had attended his wife's cooking classes? He refused Gabriel's offer to sit down and have some coffee and loomed over the table, twice as large as life. "You've been—uh—out of town till tonight, haven't you?"

"That's right." Gabriel raised an eyebrow. "You should know. After all, we asked for a house watch while we were gone." It was standard procedure in Northvale to report absences to the police, never mind that several years back a police dispatcher had orchestrated a series of burglaries of houses known to be empty.

"That's just for the record. I know you weren't home when I swung by forty-five minutes ago."

"It's clear you take house watching seriously," Gabriel said. "Everything seems to be in place, but if you'd like us to take inventory—"

"That's not why I'm here. Something's come up and—" Color flooded Tracy's face, almost submerging the freckles. "I hope you won't take offense, but I need to ask you a few questions about—" He stopped.

The mouthfuls of frittata Amelia had swallowed felt like lead in her stomach. She picked up the anonymous letter and held it out to Tracy. "About this?"

He snatched it away from her. "You got one, too? That means—" Again he stopped.

"That I didn't write it? Not necessarily. I could have sent it to myself to divert suspicion. Surely you've thought of that."

"Jeez, Mrs. Cunningham—"

"I think you'd better sit down." Gabriel got up and moved a chair behind Tracy.

"Yeah. I reckon." Tracy lowered himself into the chair gingerly, as if he were perching on a hot stove. "I'm not used to stuff like this. DWI, B and E, breaking up fights—that's what I usually handle. We're not called in for college-related stuff much, but when we are, Sergeant Green handles it. Right now he has the flu, so here I am."

"College-related stuff," Amelia echoed, in a hollow voice. "As when a member of the college community heads the list of suspects, since everybody knows about my little brainstorm in knitting class."

"Yeah. But the letters were definitely posted in Northvale and if you were out of town—"

"I might have had an accomplice. Have you thought of that?"

"Amelia!" Gabriel reached for her hand, but she jerked it away.

"Yeah." Tracy sighed. "I was afraid you'd take it like this, Mrs. Cunningham. Terry warned me you'd be real upset."

"Upset isn't the word for it." Amelia hesitated. "How many letters were there?"

"Sixteen that we know of. Seventeen, counting yours. All the same. All sent to people at the college."

"Oh my God." Amelia's insides heaved. How many more had burned their letters and were holding their breath, waiting for the world to explode? Seventeen more? Fifty? A hundred?

"Amelia, *it is not your fault!*"

"Isn't it? Who gave some sicko a blueprint for spreading misery?"

"Your husband's right, Mrs. Cunningham. You're not responsible for what happened. You didn't send the letters. If you have any idea who did, we'd appreciate—"

"No. None. Amelia pushed her plate away, put her forearms on the table, put her head down. Her heart began beating very fast. Memory cast up a stony-faced Pam Blair saying, "Don't be surprised if I plant a bomb on campus before I'm out of here." Later, when Amelia had telephoned Pam with confirmation of the worst, the reaction had been stunned silence, followed by a soft "Those bastards" that dripped with rage and venom. Could the anonymous letters have been Pam's bomb? Possibly, but they hardly seemed her style—she was up-front about everything. In any event, she wasn't the only member of the college community with a grievance. And what was to say it had to be somebody at the college? Anybody in town with an animus against gown might have seized an opportunity provided by Amelia Bigmouth. *Anybody.*

All at once she became aware that Gabriel was giving Tracy a detailed account of the trip to New York. Much too detailed for an investigation of what was, however disgusting, hardly a major crime. She jerked her head up and looked at Tracy.

"You said I wasn't responsible for what happened. What actually did happen?"

Tracy looked down at his notebook. "Somebody—uh—overreacted to the letter. Took an overdose of barbiturates."

Amelia opened her mouth, but nothing came out.

"No doubt that it was cause and effect?" Gabriel asked.

"The letter was on the table under the bottle of barbiturates she'd emptied into her coffee. Seems pretty conclusive."

Amelia found her voice. "Who?"

"Katherine Ellsworth."

Amelia's hand touched something soft and fleecy, with holes large enough to poke her fingers through. Unfamiliar, yet it was covering her. Why? She opened her eyes and discovered that she was lying on the couch, under the afghan of multicolored granny squares that was stored in the back of the closet except when Gabriel's mother, who had crocheted it, came to visit. Why was it covering her?

Memory came back in a rush. Somewhere behind her head, she heard a faint, very familiar sound—a page turning.

"Gabriel?"

"Right here." He got up from his chair and came to sit on the couch at her feet.

"Tell me I didn't swoon like a Victorian heroine."

"You did, I'm afraid. Lucky for you Tracy has some good moves—you might have cracked your head on the floor."

She freed an arm from the afghan and reached for his hand, clutched it tight, as a child clutches.

"You were out a good twenty minutes. I was almost beginning to wonder if you'd ever come out of it."

"I almost wish I hadn't."

"None of that. Sure it's awful. Nothing's going to change that. But you're not responsible, damn it!"

"No? If I hadn't opened my mouth Katherine would still be

alive, wouldn't she? How can I feel it's not my fault? How can I not feel vile?"

"Tell yourself there's somebody who must feel viler. The person who sent the letters. The portentous, voice-of-doom phraseology is a catchall. Fits everybody and doesn't even hint at anything specific. Tracy said they were all sent to people at the college. Sounds to me like another round fired in the town versus gown battle."

"You're probably right," Amelia said, and added mentally, thinking of Pam Blair again, "or somebody at the college with a grievance." She let go of Gabriel's hand and slipped her arm under the afghan so she could hug herself against a chill that seemed to be turning her insides to ice. "I agree that the letter isn't really specific enough to disturb anything but amour propre, unless you have one hell of a guilty conscience. It seems hard to believe about Katherine Ellsworth, though."

"Maybe not." Gabriel hesitated. "From the way Tracy talked, the police are satisfied she really did have something to be hot and bothered about. Not that he gave anything away, but—" A shrug. "While you were out I telephoned Bill Ellsworth and—"

"You didn't lose any time, did you?"

"For God's sake, Amelia! It was only common courtesy to offer condolences."

"Of course it was. Forgive me, darling. My head is—What did he say?"

"That she'd been extremely depressed lately. She wouldn't say why. The letter must have been the last straw."

"I suppose so. Oh God. How am I ever going to face the man again?"

"He doesn't blame you, Amelia."

"How do you know? Did he tell you to be sure and tell Amelia that he doesn't blame her?"

"No, of course not. But he made a point of thanking both of us for our concern."

"Terrific. Makes me feel like Mother Teresa."

"Christ, Amelia—"

"I know, I know. I'm being impossible." She hugged her arms tighter. "The thing is, intellectually I know you're right. But my mind and my feelings seem to belong to different people. Go to bed, Gabriel. Please. You can't help me deal with this. Nobody can."

"All right. Give a shout if you need me." Gabriel bent over to plant a kiss on her forehead and got up. The sofa cushion gave a whoosh that sounded like a sigh of relief.

Amelia listened to his footsteps on the stairs, and resentment welled up in her. There he went, off to shower and hit the sack, where he would sleep like a baby, no doubt. He was happy to abandon her to her misery.

Who could blame him?

Never mind that she'd asked him to leave her. He shouldn't have done it.

What should he have done? Stayed and reasoned with her? He'd tried that, hadn't he?

He should have tried harder.

Oh God, she was in a bad way. Was going to be in a worse one before the night was over. Always supposing the night ever would be over.

Never mind those comforting words. Gabriel believed what she believed: If she hadn't shot off her mouth first and thought second, Katherine Ellsworth might still be alive. Ergo, she was responsible for Katherine's death. No wonder he was so quick to flee upstairs. He probably couldn't stand to be around her.

Why hadn't she kept her mouth shut?

No use crying over spilt milk. No use telling herself that, either.

Katherine Ellsworth had killed herself because of the poison pen letter—that was beyond dispute. Tom Tracy had hinted to Gabriel that she'd had a guilty secret she preferred to die rather than have exposed.

What guilty secret?

Amelia groaned and burrowed deeper into the couch. The light from the lamp behind her head cast a white circle on the ceiling. A small oasis in a dark world. Reassuring. Something for a child afraid of monsters and demons and the rest of the things that go bump in the night. Which showed how much children knew about what was really scary.

She groaned again, making a prodigious amount of noise, at least to her own ears. She flung the afghan off, swung her legs to the floor, got up. No point lying there. No point going to bed, either. She would never be able to sleep.

She walked over to the kitchen area and switched on the light. The skillet with the remains of the frittata was on the stove. The dirty dishes were on the table. There was work to be done. Thank God for that.

It didn't take long. Nor did the chore that was supposed to be on tomorrow morning's agenda, removing the patina of dust that had settled over everything while they were away. She wished that she hadn't left things quite so shipshape—a dirty oven would have come in handy right now. Tackling the upstairs would have to wait until morning, unless she routed Gabriel out of bed. But at least she could make a start in the bathroom.

Gabriel had left the soggy bath mat on the floor instead of spreading it over the rim of the tub; his towel was crumpled instead of folded; the soap was lying in the middle of the tub instead of in the bamboo soap dish. All pretty much as usual. She set the place to rights in nothing flat.

All at once she felt grubby, more in need of cleaning than any part of the house. Peeling off her clothes and heaping them on the floor, she stepped into the tub and closed the shower curtain, turned on the water as hot as she could stand it. She soaped herself lavishly and scrubbed her flesh with the loofah; shampooed her hair twice; soaped and scrubbed again. She emerged from the shower red and hot, a parboiled Lady Macbeth. She dried herself off and shoved the heap of clothes into the big rattan hamper.

She tiptoed into the bedroom to collect underwear, socks, jeans, sweatshirt, tiptoed out again. Not that she needed to be all that quiet: Gabriel was sound asleep, could probably sleep through an earthquake. She returned to the bathroom, dressed hurriedly, dried her hair, and went downstairs.

It was only a quarter past two. Practically the whole night to get through. How? Pity she wasn't a drinker—she invariably got sick long before she reached oblivion, and a hangover played havoc with her intestines for days. But could she face sitting around the house cold sober and letting guilt and remorse have their way with her?

Not a chance. She had to get out of the house. Drive somewhere. Maybe out in the open, under an indifferent sky, diminished to a molecule by the towering hills, she might find the burden of responsibility diminished, too. She might even be able to put it in perspective.

Did she really believe that?

Did it matter?

She went to the closet, pulled out her old camel-hair wraparound coat, a relic of her college days and unworn for a long time. No pretending it was any warmer than her newer coats, so reaching for it had to be psychological. Security? Cocoon? Womb? It didn't bear thinking about.

The night was moonless, the mountains by starlight great dark mounds in the distance. Amelia took a route that skirted the center of town, turned onto Route 7 and headed north, toward Lake Champlain. At the back of her mind, glimmering faintly, was a hope that a combination of mountains and water would effect a miracle cure. But it was silly, she knew it was silly, and in the end she didn't go very far, pulling onto an unfamiliar side road that gave her an unobstructed view of the mountains and shutting off the engine.

The mountains were darker than the dark sky. To her sharpened night vision, they had definition now. Hills like black elephants? Hardly. Hills like hills. They had been here for centuries, would be here long after she was gone. Hold on to that thought. In comparison, she was small, she was insignificant, she was a blip in the scheme of the cosmos. All this she programmed in her mind, ran it through again and again.

It didn't help. She felt small, she felt worthless, but not for an instant did she lose sight of who she was supposed to be. Amelia Lewis Cunningham, wife of Gabriel Cunningham, assistant professor of English at Northvale College. The only crumb of comfort there was that Gabriel had tenure—having Pandora for a wife wouldn't destroy his career.

But digesting that crumb made her feel guiltier yet. What

right had she to take comfort in anything? If it hadn't been for her, Katherine Ellsworth would still be alive. Simple as that.

Of course the guilt wasn't hers alone. What must the person who bombarded Northvale College with anonymous letters be feeling now? "Another round fired in the town versus gown battle," Gabriel had said. Maybe he really was right. Plainly no aim had been taken at any specific target, but one had been hit nonetheless.

Memory stirred, cast up Katherine Ellsworth gazing at the Canton porcelain salt cellar with a look Amelia hadn't been able to interpret at the time. She could interpret it now. Whatever Katherine's guilty secret had been, it was linked to that salt.

Amelia tried to back off from that one. She couldn't possibly know that, could she? Yes. She could. She didn't know how she knew, but she did know.

Clairvoyance? If so, it was a highly selective variety, because she didn't have a clue who could have sent the letters. The idea that it might have been Pam Blair getting even for being cut loose didn't really stand up to scrutiny. She could see Pam packing up a bundle of dirty linen and taking it to the *Northvale News,* which was so staunchly anticollege that it was dubbed the "Nuisance" on campus. Or writing an angry denunciation of academic politics and publishing it under her own name. But not something as furtive and insidious as anonymous letters.

If not Pam, who? Hopeless to try to guess—tantamount to compiling a list of all Northvale's jerks, in college or out, and going eeny-meeny-miney-moe. And what difference would it make if she did know? She wouldn't feel any less guilty.

Amelia closed her eyes. A great dark cloud seemed to be pressing down on her skull, blanketing her brain cells, refusing to let them work any longer. Dark. Darker than the sky. Darker even than the mountains . . .

When she opened her eyes, the mountains were dark green against a pale gray sky. As she watched, the sky took on a lemony cast, and then, very slowly, puffs of peach-colored fleece chased each other upward and vanished. She closed her eyes again, and the next time she opened them the sun was firmly lodged in a sky that looked as if it had never been any color but blue. Time to head home.

Part
Two

5

Amelia gazed out the car window at a landscape deprived of feature by a blanket of snow. A static vista. The snow had stopped falling and the car wasn't moving. A no-no, sitting here in the middle of the road. Probably she was breaking the law, since technically the road winding up to the top of the hill was a public thoroughfare. But nothing was up there except the house, and nobody but she and Gabriel and their visitors ever used the road. She could park here all day if she liked.

She didn't like. The idea had been to get herself going. Away from home and into the world. But here she was, barely out of sight of the house, stalled. Not able to bring herself to start the engine again, to brave the unrelieved whiteness under a chilly gray-blue sky, a blanched and remote sun. The frost-laden branches of the trees seemed to bar her way. Snowy Vermont. Until she came to live in Northvale, she had taken the tag for chamber of commerce hype. Not anymore. If only it were snowing now. A good blizzard would provide a perfect excuse for burrowing in. Let it snow hard enough, long enough, and everybody might obsess about it enough to forget what she'd set in motion.

Didn't she wish. If the snow fell for forty days and forty nights, nobody would forget. Forty years might not be long enough.

How was she going to get through this?

Amelia took a deep breath; felt her seat belt press against her rib cage; exhaled slowly. It wasn't, she told herself, as if she were contemplating a major expedition. Merely a routine trip to the library and an equally routine trip to Pure Priorities. Things she had been doing a couple of times a week for years. Things she would have to go on doing a couple of times a week for the foreseeable future.

Was she going to be able to handle it?

She had to. Sooner or later. Better sooner.

She looked at herself in the rearview mirror. Saw a pale oval face, peaky in spite of the careful makeup, and all eyes. Blusher would have helped. Still, she looked presentable. Barely. She breathed deeply again and started the engine. It caught instantly. No excuse there.

The Northvale Free Library was on Principle Street, so named by the founding fathers of the town with the double-barreled aim of avoiding the overused "Main" and, via the spelling, sending a moral message to the citizenry. It was a two-story building of considerable charm, with a façade of cream stucco and mahogany trim, gabled roof and red-brick steps at the main entrance (the steps needed frequent repairs, but no one ever complained, although there was invariably bitter protest at town meetings over funds allocated to books). Inside, the somber New England rusticity of bygone years had given way to decor more suited to the age of computers and videos: pale peach walls, upholstery and curtains in bright tropical fruit colors, leaf green carpeting.

There were more people than Amelia would have liked. Three at the counter, four at the video racks, two at the shelves holding new books, three elderly men reading newspapers. Was it her imagination or did everything slow down a beat as she came in? Only a beat. And nobody actually stared—that was something.

Not enough. A good thing she had returned her last load of books to the nocturnal drop and didn't have to brave a confrontation at the counter cold turkey. She went through quickly to the stairs. Fiction and biography were on the upper level. Diversion would be there, if anywhere, and, if she had a lot of luck, no people. The first aisle, Fiction A–G, was deserted. She traversed it slowly, letting her glance flit over the shelves, knowing she was incapable of real choice. Her eyes lighted on *Nostromo,* and she pulled it off the shelf. Not her favorite Conrad, not even close, but she would go with the flow. Maybe reread *One Hundred Years of Solitude,* too—have a Latin American binge. There it was, near the end of the aisle. What else? Hudson. *The Purple Land* would do. She went to the next aisle, but found no Hudson, not even Rima the bird girl. She decided to tackle Morison's biography of Columbus, which she'd been promising herself to get to for a long time.

She walked past the other fiction aisles and reached the browsing area, with its three rectangular oak tables and no-nonsense chairs. And stopped abruptly. Someone was there. Not just any someone. Fricka McCardle, seated at the nearest table with her white head bent over a book. On a list of people Amelia wasn't ready to confront, Fricka was at the very top.

Amelia took a step backward. Not fast enough. Fricka glanced up, and a look of pure panic darkened her cornflower blue eyes. The kind of look you give a wild beast. Or a murderer. Deserved. *Deserved.* Amelia wanted to turn and flee that look, but her feet wouldn't let her—they were glued to the floor.

Fricka recovered her self-possession quickly; more than half a century of mannerly behavior had not gone for nothing. Her eyes cleared, and the smile that lifted the corners of her mouth looked almost genuine. Amelia realized, with sinking heart, how great an effort was being made.

"Amelia. I'm so glad we've run into each other. I've toyed with the idea of calling you countless times, but I was afraid of being intrusive. Believe me, I know how badly you must feel. I know you're probably blaming yourself for what happened—you wouldn't be human otherwise. You shouldn't, though. No one else does, really. Try to look on it as a tragic, tragic accident, nothing more." The almost genuine smile appeared again. "I feel it's very important that I say this to you. I also want to say that we're all looking forward to seeing you back in class very, very soon."

"Thank you," Amelia said. She excused herself from Fricka on the grounds of running late and fled into the biography section.

A tragic, tragic accident. Which would never have occurred if it hadn't been for her. As Fricka along with everyone else knew full well. That initial look of panic said it all.

How was she going to live with it? How?

She located *Admiral of the Ocean Sea* on the shelf and yanked it out, retraced her steps without looking at Fricka and carried her books downstairs to the counter. Mercifully, no one was waiting there now. Only a high-school part-time staffer to deal with. Did *she* know? Amelia didn't want to find out. She kept her eyes on her books throughout the checkout procedure and never looked at the girl's face. Adding rudeness to the rest of her sins.

She had to force herself to descend the red-brick steps at a sedate pace, walk not run to the car. She got to Pure Priorities in pretty good shape, slowed down to pull into the parking lot, and then, as the memory of Fricka McCardle's unguarded face surfaced, accelerated and drove on past.

She couldn't face it. Not yet. Not today. Practically everybody connected with Northvale College shopped at the co-op. What if she ran into some of Gabriel's colleagues in the English department? Probably she wouldn't catch anybody off guard, but guardedness wouldn't be all that much easier to take.

Something had to be done about dinner, though. Gabriel had been good about picnicking on the emergency stash in the freezer, but his patience was wearing thin and so was the stash. She decided that she would telephone Terry Tracy at the Well-Tempered Cleaver and have today's gourmet special sent over. Postpone the big food-shopping expedition till tomorrow. Or better yet, hit the Grand Union after midnight.

So okay. She was a coward. What else was new?

Amelia avoided the center of town heading home, covering distance in no time at all, zooming up the hill and around the house, shutting off the engine.

Only to discover that she couldn't bring herself to get out of the car and go into the house. Great. Just great. Not only couldn't she face other people, she couldn't face being alone with herself.

A tragic, tragic accident. Hold on to that. Hard. After all, nobody had meant for it to happen.

So what? The unmitigated truth was that somebody was dead

who would still be alive if it hadn't been for Amelia Cunningham. A truth even she couldn't dispute.

How big a jump from there to thinking of her as a murderer? How many people had made that jump?

Could she blame them?

Amelia was reading a manuscript about achieving family solidarity and posting up editorial suggestions in the margins (the one she advocated most strongly—that the entire thing be relegated to the shredder—she did not commit to paper) when the doorbell rang. The chimes resounded, went on resounding as whoever it was kept a finger on the bell. She was a bit surprised to discover what a fiendish racket chimes could make. Harder to ignore than the telephone, but not impossible.

The chiming stopped, and pounding began. "Amelia, open up. It's Millicent Neumeyer. I need to talk to you."

Amelia's heart sank. She couldn't very well ignore the wife of the president of Northvale College. She got up and went to the door. "Hello, Millicent. This is unexpected."

"And unwelcome, I've no doubt." Millicent stalked in, her big frame wrapped today in a hairy gray tweed jacket with linebacker shoulder pads and a matching skirt. She made a beeline for the sofa and sat down. "Never mind the polite disclaimers. You're going to listen to me whether you like it or not."

"Of course. Would you care for some coffee? I just made—"

"Stop stalling and sit down." Millicent patted the cushion beside her, and Amelia, feeling a bit as if she were on a leash, sat down.

"That's better. You can probably guess why I'm here, and the sooner you hear me out, the sooner I'll be out of your hair. Nobody has set eyes on you for weeks. Nobody has even heard your voice. How long do you plan to hole up like this?"

"As long as it takes."

"That's not the right answer." Millicent's large square face was hard as granite. "I've no doubt you think I enjoy dosing people with castor oil. No, don't bother to protest—your face is all too easy to read. Actually, you're quite wrong. I detest being officious. However. I won't bother to tell you that what you're doing is bad for you. You know that. What you seem to have lost sight of is that you're not just punishing yourself. You're a faculty wife, Amelia, for better or for worse, and that means your primary responsibility is not to let yourself become a liability to your husband. For God's sake, girl, stop contemplating your navel and shape up!"

"Well." Amelia took a deep breath. "That was quite a speech."

"Indeed it was. I can really grind it out when I try, can't I?" The granite face softened somewhat. "I think you're locked into bearing a burden that's really none of yours. Just imagine what life would be like if we all had to take the consequences of every idle word we utter. It puts me in mind of that baritone who gave the recital here last year, the song he sang about the Atlas with a world of woe on his shoulders. Remember how he staggered around the stage like a perfect fool?"

Amelia had to laugh. "I remember. He didn't sound nearly as bad as he looked, fortunately. It's a great song."

"Is it? I wouldn't know. I'm tone-deaf. Always have been. However. Please, Amelia, don't go on staggering under that load of woe too long. People are sympathetic to misery up to a point, and then they get bored. End of lecture. But that's not the only reason I came. I have something to tell you. About Katherine Ellsworth. It's not on the grapevine and I must rely on you not to repeat it." A heavy sigh. "I think I would like that coffee after all, thank you. Black. No sugar."

Who's stalling now? Amelia thought as she went to the coffeepot. She passed up the formality of cups and saucers for her favorite stoneware mugs, terra-cotta with black slip scrollwork and handles that could accommodate four fingers, and set them on a wicker tray; emptied half a box of wholemeal biscuits into a shallow black matte bowl; poured the coffee; carried the tray over to the sofa and put it down on the coffee table.

"Thank you." Millicent picked up her mug and sipped from it and cradled it in her hands. "About Katherine. As you may or may not know, she and Henrietta Hazelton founded the Maple

Valley Gardening Society. Henrietta used to be an avid gardener before she became housebound and she's still the titular president of the society, but in every way that matters Katherine has been running things for years. Several months ago a new treasurer took over. Young, zealous, superefficient. She discovered that the books didn't balance, some money that should have been on hand wasn't, and, for reasons I won't go into, she realized that Katherine was the only person who—"

"Oh my God. The Canton salt. That's why—" Amelia clapped a hand over her mouth.

Millicent set her mug down on the tray and raised her eyebrows. And so Amelia recounted picking up Katherine on Route 7 and being shown the Canton ware and seeing the guilty look in Katherine's eyes, incomprehensible at the time. "The salt cellar brought it there, I'm sure of that. I remember feeling almost unbearably sorry for her."

"Yes. So did we all. I expect you're right and that's where the money went. Lucy—the treasurer—felt that she couldn't simply ignore the matter, so she went to see Henrietta. Which was rather brave of her, actually. Henrietta can be quite formidable."

"So I've heard." Legend had it that in Henrietta Hazelton's veins the blood of *Mayflower* antecedents had turned to the blue of tempered steel, thus matching her personality; the wheelchair she was confined to had been mythologized into a throne, and an invitation to her rambling white mansion was like an invitation to court.

"Henrietta and Katherine went to school together, and they remained very close. Still, since Katherine was part of the college community, Henrietta consulted me. She was against confrontation—she was convinced it was a matter of yielding to overwhelming temptation and it wouldn't happen again—and for making good on the money and saying nothing. Well, I didn't think that was quite right, but the prospect of laying any more burdens on Katherine when— The point is, I didn't urge a different course on Henrietta. Eventually Katherine replaced the money—she had a small annuity—and we thought we'd done the wise thing. Now I think that if we had confronted Katherine and let her know someone else *knew,* she might not have been so vulnerable to the threat of exposure. Hindsight is always twenty-twenty, of course. You can see that you're not the only one suffering guilt pangs. I thought it only fair to tell you that."

"I—I hardly know what to say. It was very decent of you, Millicent. More than decent. Thank you."

"How much good it will do I've no idea. Stop torturing yourself, Amelia. Ultimately, Katherine was responsible for Katherine, and the sooner we all accept that the better."

Amelia sighed. "Easier said than done."

"Isn't everything." Millicent picked up her mug and drained it. "I'd like a bit more, if I may."

"Of course." Amelia took Millicent's empty mug and her own, virtually untouched, to the coffeepot, chugalugged cold coffee, refilled both mugs, and carried them back to the tray.

Millicent was munching on a biscuit. "This is a rare treat for me. Most mornings I'm at some meeting or other, and what's dished out during coffee breaks you wouldn't believe, so I pass as a coffee hater and bring my own tea bags. Please don't give me away."

Amelia smiled. "Your secret is safe with me."

Millicent did not return the smile. "I want a promise from you, Amelia. Because of the way Katherine died, the funeral was private, but there's going to be a memorial service in the college chapel a week from Sunday. Be there. Don't even think about chickening out. It won't be easy for you, but it's absolutely essential that you attend. Promise?"

Amelia promised. What choice did she have?

"One more thing. Get out of the house. Now. Deck yourself out in some swagger clothes, put on some makeup, and go. It doesn't matter where. Go and pick up some produce at Pure Priorities—they have some fine artichokes, by the way. Or go to the Vermont State Craft Center and treat yourself to a new piece of pottery." Millicent got to her feet. "I'm running late. Thank you for the coffee. Oh yes—be sure to start going to Fricka's knitting class again."

Amelia felt the stirrings of panic. "I've finished my sweater."

"Buy some more yarn and start another one."

"I'll think about it."

"Don't think about it, just do it."

When Millicent was gone, Amelia returned to her manuscript. But it was no go—she had too much to think about. Millicent had gone out of her way to be supportive. Moreover, the course she was urging was right. Which never yet in the history of the world made unwelcome counsel less unwelcome.

The thrust about letting Gabriel down had really struck home. No way Amelia could exonerate herself. She had been rationalizing her cop-out on the grounds that it didn't really matter, Gabriel had tenure. But of course it did matter. Tenure wasn't everything. He was publishing articles and blocking out a book, in hope of an associate professorship in a couple of years, a full professorship down the road, and he had every reason to hope. The last thing he needed was a wife hell-bent on turning herself into a liability. How could she have lost sight of that simple truth? Gabriel should have reminded her. Why hadn't he reminded her?

Because, of course, he would no more remind her of her obligations to him than she would remind him of his obligations to her. Because they both believed that the impetus for doing the right thing should come from within, not from without. Trust in one another was the basis of their relationship. What was his not reproaching her but proof of that trust?

She would reward that trust. She would shape up if it killed her. No more enlisting Rita, the high-school student down the road, to do her major grocery shopping and asking Terry Tracy to drop off goodies from her shop at the end of the day. No more letting the machine answer the telephone and failing to return calls. No more.

Millicent had given her excellent guidelines. First step: decking herself out. She went upstairs and got out of her house sweats. What to wear? Black slacks and a dove gray turtleneck; add her black leather jacket and it would be swagger aplenty. She washed her face and applied a light film of foundation, dabbed at her lips with lipstick, and outlined her eyes with the kohl stick (the Mata Hari look). Not ready for prime time, perhaps, but not too bad.

The phone rang when she was on her way out. She was tempted to ignore it. But no, she had just made a pledge to herself, hadn't she? Reluctantly, she went to answer. The caller was Valerie Stern, her agent. Relief produced an involuntary peal of laughter.

"Well, that's a change. Last week you were begging for work to lift you out of the dumps."

"Not really a change, I'm afraid. That was nerves. You said you would scout for a nice big project. Have you found one?"

"Shit, yes. It's big all right." A pause, and Amelia heard, over the wire, the click of the cigarette lighter Val could never get to work the first time. "It's also garbage. Some woman who claims to be in touch with the spirits of dead celebrities has committed their messages to paper."

"Sounds like what inquiring minds want to know."

"More or less. Sentimentality rather than smut, though. How Marilyn Monroe loved her teddy bear, how Steve McQueen put together his first hot rod, stuff like that. I can see a market beyond the checkout counter. Remember that woman in England who claimed to be in touch with the great composers and gave concerts of the music they passed on to her? She filled concert halls for a while. This gal's English, too. Living in L.A. now. Where else would she be living? The script needs a lot of work, mostly to make the voices sound reasonably different. There'll be a small percentage for you, but it probably won't be enough. Nothing could be."

"Wow. You really know how to sell, Val."

"That's my job. Actually, I can't think of anybody better than you for it—they're over the moon about the I-remember-Reagan manuscript—and you did say you're desperate for work. Something I should mention is that one of the celebrities is Amelia Earhart, your mother's idol. Is that a turnon or a turnoff?"

Amelia said she wasn't sure, and they both laughed. Val said she would send the manuscript via overnight mail, and Amelia hung up feeling immeasurably grateful to Val for providing work on demand, no questions asked. A ton of manuscripts, outlines, and whatnot to evaluate, and now this loony tunes editorial project that would require maximum concentration and cut down drastically on brooding time. How strange that it should be Val proving such a friend in need. Years ago, when they had both worked as researchers on the same magazine, they hadn't been particularly tight because, Amelia had to admit, she had found Val's pushiness rather trying.

The artichokes at Pure Priorities were, as promised, very fine. Where they came from out of season Amelia didn't know and didn't care. She bought eight, to be cooked in two batches and eaten over the next four days—there was nothing Gabriel enjoyed more than an artichoke vinaigrette at room temperature. She also bought veal scallops and lemons for her primitive version of veal piccata, which was a long way from the real thing but very tasty; new potatoes to cook and serve in their skins with butter and chopped parsley; fresh spinach; fresh raspberries and crème fraîche. At the checkout counter she exchanged smiles and hellos with a college librarian whose name she didn't know; not until she was in the car buckling up did it dawn on her that the encounter was exactly the sort of thing she'd been dreading.

A giant step forward had been taken, clearly. And there would be a terrific dinner on the table tonight—a start at making amends to Gabriel for what she had been putting him through lately. He had been endlessly patient with her, talking it out and talking it out, saying all the right things, the logical things, the supportive things. Apart from anything else, he had to be bored out of his gourd with the whole business by now.

As soon as she got home, she put four of the artichokes in a pot with water and started them cooking, washed the raspberries and the potatoes carefully and the spinach extra carefully. While she was pounding the veal, another way of making amends occurred to her. She would knit Gabriel a sweater. In New York she had worn the olive green box-weave sweater a lot and he had admired it, hinting that he wouldn't object to having one like it. Well, of course he could have one like it, but couldn't she do even better second try? She remembered that the Northvale yarn shop had some machine-washable Italian wool in a wonderful shade of maroon. Armed with that and a more complicated pattern than the one she had followed before, she would have a good reason for returning to Fricka McCardle's knitting class, thereby killing two birds with one stone.

So, wonder of wonders, she found herself making two excursions into the world in one day. The maroon yarn was still in stock, the color every bit as good as she remembered, and she found a pattern for a man's crew-neck sweater alternating basic cables and panels of seed stitch. Manageable for the next-to-novice knitter, according to the shop's proprietress; once the cable technique was mastered, the trick was to place markers between the cables and the seed stitch panels to avoid confusion. Remembering how much trouble seed stitch had given Shannon Fiore, Amelia wasn't entirely convinced, but facing a challenge wouldn't hurt any.

Dinner was a triumph. Had the artichokes been less succulent, the veal less savory, the raspberries and cream less sumptuous, dinner would nonetheless have been a triumph. Because Amelia had the happy inspiration to dress up in the mauve silk chiffon dress that was Gabriel's favorite. Greeting him at the door, she watched his expression change from the wary neutrality all too familiar of late, to incredulity, to relief, to joy. They dined by candlelight. Women's-magazine stuff, but it worked. Over the meal they reminisced about the many candlelight dinners they had shared in London, when they had had to economize to stretch Gabriel's grant to the utmost and were never any the worse for it. Later, things got even better. They made eager, uninhibited love, first on the sofa, then on the floor, and way, way into the small hours, in bed.

Long after Gabriel fell into an exhausted sleep, Amelia lay wide awake. Her thoughts were whirling. For once, though, she didn't mind, because they were a carryover from the earlier table talk. Pleasant to remember what a good time they had had during that year in London, when they had spent so many days in the British Museum reading about Dante Gabriel Rossetti, that exotic, bizarre Victorian figure who might have found himself at home in Greenwich Village a hundred years later. The premise of Gabriel's dissertation was that Rossetti, with his enthusiasm for blue china, wombats, wallabies, and curiosities of all sorts, his wild mood swings from the self-loathing that induced him to bury a volume of his poems with his wife to the self-love that induced him to dig them up again, his dissipations and his paranoia, symbolized the doubts, the spiritual malaise, the loss of awe and wonder and mystery that went with the breakup of faith in the latter half of the nineteenth century. And the dissertation had been brilliant, synthesizing the nebulous elements of thought and feeling of the age with precision, clarity, and wit; promoting Gabriel into a plum job with a rapid tenure track. Amelia had been proud to share the load of research, to contribute to achieving a mutually desired goal.

All at once a picture popped into her head: Max Beerbohm's cartoon of the young Dante Gabriel Rossetti stretched out under a table, sketching, sublimely indifferent to his father and an assortment of exiled Italian patriots firing political salvos over his head. A picture worth a thousand dissertations?

No. Of course not. Damned if she would allow everything in her entire universe to go sour on her!

She looked over at Gabriel's face, only inches away from hers. In the faint moonlight squeezing in through the shutters, he looked contented and untroubled. She stroked his cheek, felt the start of beard against the pale olive skin. He didn't wake. He seldom woke once he had fallen asleep.

Tenderness washed over her. She loved him. God, how she loved him. To spare him any further anxiety, she would walk on eggs if she had to. Whatever it took.

6

When Amelia made her return to knitting class, she wore the olive green box-weave sweater, which proved one of her happier inspirations. The praises of style, color, workmanship, while doubtless overdone (Fricka commended the assembly of the garment as "neat and professional looking"), seemed to carry everybody over a giant hump. Amelia found herself wanting to catch Suzanne's eye. Force of habit. Suzanne wasn't there.

Where was she? Absent for the day or a dropout? Amelia couldn't very well ask, since the others knew she and Suzanne were close. She felt a pang at having neglected Suzanne lately— one more thing to feel guilty about. But of course Suzanne would understand.

Fricka got Amelia started on the maroon sweater, sorted everybody else out, and all seemed as usual. Lots of small talk, amiable enough. Shannon Fiore told of some acquaintances in Montpelier who were planning to circulate a mail-order catalog aimed at grandparents; this touched off a dippy-small-businesses-I-have-heard-about contest and led, almost inevitably, to Ruth Davidson's hilarious critique of the film in which Diane Keaton, new to Hollywood's fantasy version of Vermont, makes big bucks marketing gourmet baby food. Everyone seemed relaxed, genial, accepting of Amelia's presence without making a big deal of it. There was only one awkward moment. Fricka left the room to answer the telephone, and Christine Gotkowski said, "You can see she thinks she has a clear field now." General laughter, giving way, after furtive glances at Amelia, to embarrassment. Then Fricka returned, and Elvira Chan launched into an account of a fashion show she had attended on her last visit to New York, a cross between son-et-lumière and a sixties happening. What Christine's remark, the laughter, and the embarrassment were all about Amelia didn't know and felt she could bear not knowing.

At the end of class, Fricka asked Amelia to stay a few minutes longer "so we can be sure problems won't creep up with that pattern." That this wasn't the real reason Amelia knew, but she couldn't refuse. Because Fricka had, that day at the library, proved human and let her guard down for a moment, exposing her true feelings, she felt she had to make up for it, and Amelia had to let her.

Sure enough. "I'm not really concerned that you can't handle the pattern," Fricka said. "I wanted to talk to you. Partly to tell you that I'm glad you've come back to class. Mostly, though, to tell you what I'm sure you can't hear often enough. Katherine's death was not your fault. Even those who were closest to her don't hold you responsible. You might be capable of uttering a cutting remark in the heat of the moment, but the sort of calculating maliciousness that concocts such a cruel, cruel letter and satirically addresses the victim as Esquire—I mean Ms., of course—well, it simply isn't in you, Amelia. No one who knows you at all could possibly believe it is." And Fricka leaned forward to brush lavender-scented lips against Amelia's cheek. Amelia was touched and, in spite of herself, amused at this truly Victorian sendoff. She wished Suzanne were there to see it.

Over the course of the next few days, Amelia thought about telephoning Suzanne, but each time she brought herself nearly to the brink she pulled back. Initiating contact with anyone in Northvale, even Suzanne, was simply too daunting. She told herself that it didn't much matter, Suzanne would understand. Anyway, she would see Suzanne at the commemorative service for Katherine Ellsworth, and they could sort things out then.

But when Amelia and Gabriel were seated in Prendergast Memorial Chapel for the service, Suzanne was nowhere in sight. Amelia let her eyes wander, picked out William Ellsworth, pale and patrician in charcoal tweed, every inch the grieving widower, seated in the front row next to Millicent Neumeyer. She lowered her head, reminded of the solemnity of the occasion, realizing with some surprise that this was the first time she had ever entered the chapel for the sort of function it had been built for; on every other occasion she had attended a performance of some sort. It was a soothing place. Flat white walls, tawny hardwood wall paneling, tawny hardwood benches, parquet floor, mullioned windows with frosted glass, streamlined contemporary organ, the ambience of here rather than hereafter challenged (but not much) by a bronze cross set among the organ pipes and by hymnal racks on the benches. Amelia wondered which of the Northvale ministers would preside over the service.

No minister came through the door associated, in Amelia's mind, with the entrance of singers and dancers and instrumentalists. Instead, a woman in a wheelchair rolled herself across the stage. Short, feathery white tendrils of hair framed a face with strong chin, Roman emperor's nose, and large, piercing eyes almost as dark as the black cashmere shawl fastened at her left shoulder with a diamond brooch. Henrietta Hazelton. She said "Good morning" in a deep, somewhat raspy contralto that resonated through the chapel (absurdly, Amelia was reminded of her mother's description of Ethel Merman in *Annie Get Your Gun:* "You could hear every word she sang in the last row of the balcony—solid brass in every register") and launched without preamble into a tribute to Katherine Ellsworth. She spoke of a young faculty wife who came to Northvale from Boston imbued with the ideal of community service; who was instrumental in obtaining nutritious lunches for schoolchildren, community aid for unwed mothers and battered wives, transport for the elderly; who lobbied tirelessly against dumping toxic wastes and wanton destruction of trees. The contralto softened considerably as Henrietta Hazelton went on to relate that Katherine Ellsworth had loved all growing things, that she had been renowned as a gardener, that she had been one of the founders of the Maple Valley Gardening

Society and helped to raise gardening above the level of hobby. "Those of us who valued Katherine know exactly what we have lost." Abruptly, the wheelchair made an about-face and rolled off the stage more rapidly than it had rolled on.

Silence. Then the organ embarked on the "St. Anne Chorale," the sound swelling majestically through the chapel. The commemorative service was over. For a moment or two, nobody seemed to believe it, and then, discreetly, against the backdrop of the music, talking began. "Amazing," Gabriel murmured. "In and out in the twinkling of an eye. Who'd have thunk it?"

People started moving. A crowd began to form around William Ellsworth. Gabriel propelled Amelia toward it. ("We can't duck this." "I know.") Waiting to offer condolences, Amelia felt numb, hollow, as if she had passed on to some parahuman plane beyond trepidation, anxiety, guilt. Would this detachment survive the faintest whiff of animosity? It wasn't put to the test. When she told William Ellsworth how sorry she was about Katherine, he was his usual courteous self, and the way he pressed the hand she offered went beyond courtesy. If she hadn't been locked into that other plane, she might have burst into tears.

On the way out, they encountered Enrico and Silvia Bianchi with tall, rangy Hal Longman in tow, minus Suzanne. In response to enquiry, Hal said Suzanne had "one of her migraines" and hadn't felt up to coming. Amelia expressed her sympathy. Silvia, with one of her calculated spontaneous gestures, embraced Amelia and said, "Dinner soon. I'll call you." Amelia went home convinced that Millicent Neumeyer was right. People didn't hold her responsible for Katherine's death. Or, if they did, they were more than willing to cultivate amnesia. She resolved that she would do her damnedest to cultivate amnesia, too.

The resolution lasted two days. Until she pulled into the service station on Maple Street for gas and spotted Suzanne Longman's bronze Subaru in the next lane. Suzanne was in the driver's seat, and, as Amelia started to roll down her window, the Subaru started up and zoomed out of the station. A blast of exhaust fumes assaulted her like a blow.

Well, it was a blow, wasn't it? Or a slap in the face, at the very least. How could Suzanne not have seen her? Face it. Suzanne had seen her and fled. That hurt.

Amelia had planned a a visit to the Vermont State Craft Center to buy a set of stoneware bowls she had been tempted by a couple of months ago and passed up because of the price. This morning she had suddenly remembered them and decided she wanted them. A good sign, wanting something. A commitment of sorts, or at least a willingness to get on with it. But the snub from Suzanne had knocked her back to square one. She drove out of the service station and headed back home, knowing that it was the wrong thing to do, not caring that it was the wrong thing to do.

Why had Suzanne cut her? Now that she came to think of it, Suzanne wasn't one of the people who had tried to reach her of late and had been forced to talk to the machine. Strange that she hadn't wondered about it before. No, not strange. If a polka-dot kangeroo had shown up on the doorstep she wouldn't have wondered about it or about anything else. So okay. Suzanne hadn't tried to get in touch with her and, at the first accidental encounter, had turned tail and run. What did that mean? The obvious explanation was that Suzanne blamed her for Katherine's death and was trying to avoid her.

But Amelia balked at the obvious. Suzanne was a friend. She had understood the impulse that had provoked those devastating words in knitting class. She had made light of the whole thing, even laughing at Amelia's remorse. Had the transformation of that ill-advised flight of fancy into reality turned Suzanne off completely? A distinct possibility with someone less sophisticated. But Suzanne? Maybe the real Suzanne was somebody Amelia didn't know.

Or maybe Suzanne really thought Amelia had sent the anonymous letters. How likely was that? No one else did, not even the police. Or did they? Maybe they took the line that what you can't prove, sweep under the rug. That was the way things worked in a town the size of Northvale. That was the way they had to work. Otherwise how could anybody face anybody else?

Don't think like that, she told herself. *Ever*. Think positive. She *had* to think positive. For Gabriel's sake, if not her own.

Act positive, for starters. Find out why Suzanne had cut her. There had to be a reason.

The minute she got home, she went to the phone and punched out Suzanne's number. And got Hal's voice on the answering machine. She hung up without leaving a message. She would try again later. In the meantime, she would get on with the day as planned.

At the craft center, the stoneware bowls had not been sold, and they were every bit as beautiful as Amelia remembered. A set of three nesting bowls, each shaped like an inverted beehive, the color of wet sand with a plain matte glaze. As before, she winced at the price tag, but decided what the hell, there was nothing like extravagance to make you feel you'd rejoined the human race. She wrote out a check, accepted a card with the potter's name and address (in case she broke a bowl, which God forbid), and passed up a state-of-the-art shopping bag in favor of a battered box tied with twine. She told herself that the purchase made her feel better—and totally failed to believe it.

Heading home, Amelia chose a roundabout route that took her past the Longmans' house. The Subaru was in the driveway. She drove on by, reversed, backed up in front of the house, stopped the car. From the front, the house looked no larger than her own, but in back the Longmans had added a two-story extension half the size of the original house and beyond that a glass-roofed patio. Lots of space, Amelia thought as she walked up to the door, for Suzanne to lose herself if she chose not to answer the doorbell.

But Suzanne came to the door. Slightly gray in the face, the wonderful russet hair straggling out of the usually impeccable chignon, looking as if the migraine Hal said she was suffering from had lasted a month.

"Come in." Not welcoming. Not hostile either. Resigned.

"You look like hell, Suzanne. I suppose the decent thing to do would be bow out gracefully and wait for an explanation until you're feeling better, but decency's beyond me these days. You saw me at the gas station. I *know* you saw me. So why? Not that I haven't guessed."

"Yes. I thought you probably had." Suzanne turned her back

and glided gracefully down the hall in her jeans and sweatshirt and Nikes, a princess in goosegirl's clothes.

Amelia followed, past the living room and Hal's study, to the kitchen that comprised the entire ground floor of the house extension, a room full of light from picture windows on two sides and french windows opening onto the patio. All at once the smell of chili assaulted her nostrils and she went weak in the knees, barely making it to the bench alongside the redwood trestle table where she always sat. Suzanne was already seated opposite in her usual place. Sideways, no doubt so she didn't have to look at Amelia.

Guilt, remorse, all the misery that Amelia had been trying to bury came welling up afresh. "Damn it, Suzanne, I thought we were friends! So okay, none of this would have happened if I'd had sense enough to keep my big mouth shut. God knows I've tormented myself every which way about it. But can I really be blamed because some nutcase picked up my idiot idea and ran with it? I was absolutely devastated when you made it so plain that you did blame me, that you wanted to distance yourself from such a worthless wretch. *You,* of all people. I thought you understood that I never meant—"

Amelia stopped. Because Suzanne's shoulders were shaking. Because Suzanne was emitting harsh, strident sounds. Because— incredibly—Suzanne was *laughing.*

"Oh, Amelia. Oh, Amelia. Poor, sweet Amelia. For such a bright woman you can be awfully thick at times."

"What the hell is that supposed to mean?"

"Don't you know? Don't you have even the tiniest inkling? I guess not. Maybe it's not stupidity. Maybe it's just simple egotism that can't think beyond blows to self-esteem." Suzanne's shoulders were rigid now, as she gazed out at the glass-enclosed patio, which was virtually her private space, part greenhouse, part studio. "It's almost funny, you know. Here you are, so concerned about losing my good opinion, when all the time I've dreaded facing you. I was sure you must have guessed."

"Guessed? Guessed what? I don't have a clue—" Amelia stopped. The beat of her heart accelerated, way ahead of her mind. "Oh my God, Suzanne. *You?* I can't believe—"

Again Amelia stopped, as Suzanne turned around in her seat, exposing a haggard face that looked a score of years older than the familiar one. And all at once Amelia did believe. The afternoon in knitting class flashed through her brain like a tape. Ruth Davidson's irritation at the smug self-satisfaction of the academic community, Suzanne's support, the indignation of the others, her own facetious attempt to shut them all up, the way they had all turned on her. Except Suzanne. Suzanne had made fun of the whole business, pooh-poohed her remorse, called the idea "dynamite" and "diabolically clever," all of which she had taken at the time for an attempt to console her. Not anymore. Christ, not anymore.

Why, during the hours and hours of wild speculation, had the truth never once occurred to her? Suzanne must be right—she hadn't been able to think past her wounded self-esteem. Otherwise she would have guessed, suspected, *something.* But no, she'd been too busy beating her breast and shouting *mea culpa* to spare a thought for the motivation behind the letters. Then, too, she hadn't believed there was anything to think about. Like everybody else, she had accepted the prevailing theory of vendetta, whether town versus gown or academic infighting; had visualized the letter writer as some embittered soul with a grievance. Wrong, wrong, wrong. All the letter writer had done was follow through on a demented blueprint for letting air out of some overinflated balloons.

Which meant that all the breast-beating, all the wallowing in guilt, had been warranted. Wasn't she the architect, after all?

"No, Amelia." Suzanne's lip curled in the familiar half smile. "I can read your thought processes on your face. Step by step. And no, dear, you are not equally guilty."

"I think I am. I think it's more or less a *folie à deux.*"

Suzanne shrugged. "Have it your way. Doesn't much matter, does it?"

"I suppose not. Suzanne, if you don't mind—I think I'd just about kill for a cup of coffee right now."

"Of course. Sorry." And Suzanne got up and went to the stove on the cooking island in the middle of the room, under pots and pans and various cooking utensils that hung from black iron hooks emerging from a central axis like the tentacles of a giant centipede, and started the familiar ritual.

Amelia took a deep breath. "One thing I'm curious about. How did you select your targets? By sticking a pin in the college directory?"

Suzanne met her gaze levelly. "It was more personal than that. Most of the people I chose had it coming. Not you, naturally—I threw you in because I knew you'd be at the top of the suspect list. I threw in a few more blameless souls as well, for balance and to lend a Halloween air to the proceedings." The lower lip curled. "Now you're about to ask me whether I targeted Katherine Ellsworth as one of the sinners or one of the saints. Don't."

"Suzanne—"

"I said don't!" Suzanne took down a pair of mugs and clacked them down on the counter. "I'm not ready to deal with that yet."

The coffeemaker gurgled. The two of them listened intently, as if the sound were of world-shaking importance. Sooner or later, Amelia thought, Suzanne was going to have to come to terms with her guilt or go round the bend. A patent truth. She didn't voice it. Suzanne certainly knew it better than anybody else.

The coffeemaker stopped gurgling. Suzanne filled the mugs and brought them to the table along with an empty saucer. She sat down, took a packet of Pall Malls out of her pocket, shook out a cigarette, lit up, inhaled deeply, exhaled slowly. A thin column of smoke rose above her head.

"I didn't know you smoked."

"I don't. Not for years. Hal would have a fit if he knew. He won't find out. I buy my cigarettes in Burlington, I gargle a lot, and lately I've been treating him to his Tex-Mex favorites, which are pungent enough to submerge any other smells." Suzanne took another deep drag on the cigarette. "Christ! I've never felt so boxed in. That's what it's all about, you know. Being boxed in. You know I grew up on a ranch in New Mexico?"

Amelia nodded.

"Everything's so different there. All spread out, including the people. Georgia O'Keeffe got it right. A lot of the time you're the only thing between earth and sky—nothing but space around you.

When I was a little girl, I used to spend entire days in the saddle, roaming around by myself or with my Navajo buddies, shooting my lunch more often than not. I thought everybody lived like that. I hooked up with Hal when he was doing research on the pueblos, and ever since I've found myself in places where there are lots of people jockeying for position, playing mickey mouse politics from morning to night. You'd think I would have adjusted to life within a pecking order by now, wouldn't you? But I haven't. Every so often I feel if I don't do something to shake up the piles of bird-seed and bird shit, I'll explode. So I do something." The lower lip curved in the half smile.

"Such as?"

Suzanne drew smoke into her lungs and crushed out her cigarette in the saucer. "Such as the time the one and only Edith Selden Van Vliet bullied the faculty wives into preparing a gala dinner for blue-blood/blue-chip alumni and there was a stampede for the toilets. They never figured out it was Ex-Lax in the chocolate mousse."

Amelia had to smile. "That was you? I heard about that dinner party even before I came to Northvale. Sticking it to Edith Van Vliet made an awful lot of people happy. But didn't the Northvale alumni fund suffer?"

"Oh, sure. Fewer scholarships for *Mayflower* descendants, WASP tennis players, and such like. That's serious damage, I suppose."

Serious damage. The words seemed to reverberate, sobering them both up fast.

"Quit castigating yourself, Amelia. If I hadn't pulled this, it might have been something worse."

"Nothing could be worse."

Flat. Bald. Incontrovertible. The words hung leaden in the air. Amelia would have given anything to unsay them.

"I'm sorry, Suzanne. That was stupid. I know you didn't intend to do real harm. You couldn't have known Katherine had a guilty secret. I suppose it's like throwing darts at random and happening to hit an artery. Not that it isn't wrong to throw darts, but—"

"Oh, Amelia." And Suzanne started to laugh again, emitting

the same raucous, mirthless sounds as before. This time the seizure left her gasping for breath.

"All right. I suppose that did sound a little facile. But it wasn't just cheap consolation, I really do think Katherine's death was a ghastly accident. I can't believe you deliberately targeted that sad sack of a woman."

"You're right there. She wasn't one of my sinners. But she wasn't one of my saints either. I never sent her a letter at all."

"What?"

"I didn't send the letter to her, I sent it to *him."*

"Him? You mean William?" Incredulity made Amelia's voice shrill.

"Yes, the noble William. Mr. Perfect. Mr. Perfect Bastard is more like it. You're shocked, I see. Obviously he's got you bamboozled, too."

"It would seem so. You've lost me, Suzanne. I've never heard anything discreditable about William Ellsworth."

"Haven't you? Nobody's ever told you that he makes a career of banging his students? I'm not talking occasional fling, I'm talking calculation. Every year he picks out some sweet young thing and sweeps her off her feet, cons her into believing she's in some great romantic nirvana, and at the end of spring term he treats her to a poignant parting, full of noble sentiments about how an old crock with commitments can't take up any more of her life. So she spends her summer vacation dreaming of ways to get him back, because of course he's convinced her the parting is for her sake, only to find him regretful but adamant. If she's lucky, she'll file the whole thing away in her memory bank and get on with her life. If she's not, she'll keep on caring, pick up on the next conquest, and feel as if she's been sandbagged." Bitterness rang through Suzanne's voice. "You should pay more attention to gossip, Amelia."

"This sounds like something more than gossip."

"It is." Suzanne lit another cigarette; drew smoke into her lungs. "My daughter Sara. Oh, she wasn't a virgin, but it had all been puppy play, nothing serious. She didn't have a chance against William. He's clever. He lets the girl make the running, so she has nobody to blame but herself. Sara was utterly devastated when he dropped her. Moped around the house, couldn't eat, couldn't sleep, even tried—She had to transfer to another college because she couldn't bear to stay in Northvale. I feel I lost her sooner than I should have. I've hated William Ellsworth ever since. A girl's first romantic experience shouldn't be with a dirty old man, damn it! Under all that country squire graciousness and charm, that's what he is—a dirty old man."

Amelia didn't know what to say. That a young girl should have her first meaningful sexual experience with an older, civilized man didn't sound so awful. What were the alternatives? More often than not, some callow big man on campus who notched the bedpost or some scruffy antiestablishment specimen selected to spite Mommy and Daddy. Well, maybe that was a bit cynical. Still, she found it hard to believe that William Ellsworth was as calculating as Suzanne claimed. Even if he had been around the block a few times too many, he was a more than presentable aging man with a wife who had let herself turn into an unattractive lump. As a college professor, he had unlimited access to nubile nymphs, and it was a commonplace that seductions went with the territory. Not something any faculty wife liked to think about (thank God she'd never had reason to think about it herself), but the possibility was always there.

"You think I'm making a big deal out of a routine campus seduction." Suzanne's tone was flat, empty.

"Well, I was sort of wondering. But of course I'm not a mother."

"That's right. You're not."

Dismissive. Justified? Maternity was a club that Amelia had elected not to join, Gabriel being set against children and she herself having no desire for the patter of little feet. The conventional wisdom notwithstanding, she had never felt a lack (which was not to say she wouldn't years from now). Nor did she feel unfit to evaluate any situation involving a child. She had always found Sara Longman a level-headed, well-adjusted girl, full of enthusiasm for her work as junior counsel in a Philadelphia law firm that did a lot of pro bono work. If her heart had been broken, it seemed to have mended pretty well.

"All right. I'm your basic overprotective mother." Suzanne

sighed. "If I could wrap my girls in cotton wool and guide them through their lives unscathed, I'd sell my soul to do it. I admit it. You can't imagine what it's cost me to give them space to grow up in, but I've done it. Read the psychology manuals till the words blurred in front of my eyes, busted my tail to be a friend to them instead of a warden, never let them suspect I was bursting with smother love. Sometimes I think Hal must know Laid-back, Everything's-cool Mom is all a bluff, but he's never called me on it, even though it's forced him into the role of heavy at times. Never mind. I got the job done. They both turned out pretty well."

"Better than that," Amelia said, with sincerity. "For God's sake, Suzanne, if you start second-guessing yourself about everything you'll go nuts!" She took a deep breath. "Look, let's make a pact right now. To stop thinking about it, stop flagellating ourselves. I mean really, *really* stop. Neither one of us meant harm to anybody. What happened to Katherine was an accident. Dreadful, but an accident."

Suzanne's face went stony, and her eyes were suddenly unfathomable. "Was it?"

"It had to be. If you addressed the letter to William, Katherine must have opened it by mistake and her guilt feelings about—whatever guilty secret she had sent her over the edge. That has to be the explanation. What other explanation could there be?"

Suzanne puffed at her cigarette, saying nothing.

A cold vise gripped the pit of Amelia's stomach. "All right. What is it you haven't told me?"

Still Suzanne was silent, puffing steadily, sending up a column of smoke. Then: "Remember how the envelope of your letter was addressed?"

"Yes. To *Ms.* Amelia Cunningham. So what? I'll bet most of Katherine's mail was addressed to Mrs. William Ellsworth, and she could easily have misread—"

"No. And it wasn't a typo, either. I addressed the envelope to William Ellsworth, Esquire. All the letters I sent to men were addressed that way."

Something stirred in the depths of Amelia's mind. She realized that "Esquire" wasn't a total surprise. Had Tom Tracy mentioned it? Not that it mattered.

"Maybe you slipped up once."

"I didn't. I checked all the envelopes before I sent them. There isn't the remotest chance that Katherine opened the envelope by mistake."

"What are you trying to say?"

"I'm saying that the bastard killed her. I'm saying that between us we left a loaded gun lying around, and he picked it up and used it. There's no other explanation."

"There must be. Suzanne—"

"Go home, Amelia." Suzanne stubbed out her cigarette, swung her legs out from under the table, and turned her back on Amelia. Folding her arms across her chest, she stared out at the patio. "I can't talk about it anymore. I can't think about it anymore."

Amelia knew she should say something, there were lots of things to say. She didn't say any of them. She got up, left the kitchen, went through the hall, opened the front door. Stepping across the threshold, she almost called out the usual "See you later," and was hard put to suppress it. Normalcy is a tough habit to break.

7

Let me get this straight, Mrs. Cunningham." Incredulity in Tom Tracy's voice. "You're asking me to tell you how the envelopes of the anonymous letters were addressed?"

"I know what you're going to say. You're going to say it's none of my business, and of course you'd be perfectly right but— You see, I've really been agonizing over this, and—surely you can understand that. I feel that if I could just get a fix on the sort of person who sent the letters I can begin to put the whole thing behind me and—The one I got was addressed to *Ms*. Amelia Cunningham. I'd guess that envelopes to men would have been addressed without any courtesy title. Like, say, 'Thomas Tracy.' " Amelia gripped the receiver of the telephone a little tighter. "Am I right?"

"Mrs. Cunningham—"

"It's still none of my business, that goes without saying. But still, I can't see that it would do any harm to tell me, and it would set my mind at rest. It can hardly be classified information, after all."

"I guess not." A deep sigh came over the wire. "Wild speculation isn't much use in a police investigation, Mrs. Cunningham. As a matter of fact, all the men's letters turned over to us had 'Esquire,' abbreviated, after the names on the envelopes."

"Really? How sarcastic." The word reverberated oddly in Amelia's brain, like an echo. "It completely changes my image of the person who sent the letters. Makes it more malicious mockery than vendetta, somehow. At least to my mind." She took a deep breath: now or never. "The thing I stick at is somebody having the gall to address a pillar of the community like Katherine Ellsworth as 'Ms.' Just out of curiosity, was her envelope really addressed that way?"

"I can't tell you that."

"Can't or won't?"

"Can't." Tracy sounded more than a little exasperated. "She got rid of the envelope. We only found the letter. Almost torn in half, like she started to get rid of that, too, but thought better of it."

"Oh." Amelia's heart plummeted to the pit of her stomach.

"Look, Mrs. Cunningham, we shouldn't be having this conversation. You know that as well as I do."

"Right. We never had it. Thank you for your patience. However absurd my curiosity may seem, it was like an itch that wouldn't go away."

"I understand how you feel. Do yourself a favor, Mrs. Cunningham. Quit punishing yourself. What good does it do?"

On that all too familiar refrain the conversation ended. Amelia replaced the receiver, her fingers almost numb from gripping it so tightly. She flexed and kept on flexing her hand until the feeling came back. Too bad the rest of her wasn't that easy to deal with. She felt taut, overwound. It had been hard work, coming on like a ditzy busybody, assuming a totally alien personality. No Mata Hari she—deception was too repugnant. But what other way was there? She could hardly have asked directly about matters of official police business and expected to receive answers. Surely the end justified the corkscrew means: she had those answers.

So okay. Now she knew for sure that the anonymous letters to men had been addressed "Esq.," thereby dispelling any doubts of Suzanne's veracity.

Had she really entertained any doubts?

Never mind. She knew for sure that no envelope had been

found with the anonymous letter everyone assumed had been sent to Katherine. Go from there.

Go where? To the conclusion that Katherine's death was murder, not suicide?

Not necessarily. There were other possibilities.

Such as?

Maybe Suzanne had misaddressed the envelope, in spite of her certainty that she hadn't.

How likely was that?

Or maybe Katherine had been in the habit of opening her husband's mail, and it was his disgrace she couldn't live with, not her own.

How likely was that?

How likely was it that William Ellsworth was a murderer?

But of course she knew diddly about what William Ellsworth was or wasn't—Suzanne's revelations had proved that much. Of all the professors she would have tagged as campus seducers, William Ellsworth was far down the list. Still, with a wife like Katherine—

There she went again, finding excuses for him. Because he was so damned charming, no doubt. Hadn't he charmed her out of that freshly baked gingerbread when she knew baking another would keep her up half the night? Yes, she could easily imagine him charming the pants or the panty hose off anybody. As for Katherine's letting herself go, well, which came first, the chicken or the egg? A chronically philandering husband might make any woman give up on making the most of herself, seek gratification in her garden and in Canton porcelain.

Would such a woman turn to suicide rather than face having the secrets of her boudoir revealed to the world at large? It strained credulity a bit, but it was possible.

Anything was possible—the problem in a nutshell. The police and all of Northvale believed Katherine Ellsworth had committed suicide. Suzanne believed William Ellsworth had murdered his wife. Which? There was no way of knowing for sure.

Amelia suddenly realized she was hugging her arms tightly enough to cut off the circulation. She relaxed her grip and massaged her upper arms.

Suicide or murder? However wretched she had been before over Katherine's death, she felt worse now. As if she might explode if she didn't find out the truth.

Ridiculous. There was no way she could find out the truth. Was there?

Amelia got up and stretched. If she were Kinsey Millhone or V. I. Warshawski, she would go out for a long run and, at the end of it, hey presto! her brain would supply her with the right questions to ask and the clever ways to ask them.

Such as: By the way, William, did you murder your wife?

8

Dear Mrs. Hazelton,

This is a very painful letter to write; it will, I'm afraid, be equally painful for you to read.

As you probably know—as everyone in Northvale probably knows—a witticism manqué of mine spawned the anonymous letters that led to Katherine Ellsworth's death. I didn't write the letters, but I couldn't feel much worse if I had. Any number of people have told me I'm not responsible for what happened, my own reason has told me I'm not responsible, and yet, in my heart, I find it impossible to absolve myself.

In brief, I've been tormented by remorse. I would gladly rationalize it away if I could, but I can't. Somehow, I must come to terms with my culpability. Before I can do that, I need to understand, intellectually and emotionally, the extent of Katherine Ellsworth's vulnerability. Therefore I appeal to you, her close friend for so many years, and ask whether you would be willing to talk to me about her.

Very likely you regard this request as presumptuous in the extreme. For all I know you could be thinking that I deserve to be every bit as wretched as I am and that it's none of yours to help me work through my guilt. If so, I can't say that I blame you.

Sincerely,
Amelia Cunningham

Dear Mrs. Cunningham:
I will see you Thursday next at 5 P.M.

Henrietta Hazelton

The house stood tall, three stories and an attic, looking down on the world, as befitted a manor house. White clapboard exterior (real wood, Amelia was willing to bet, not the aluminum facsimile). Door, window frames, shutters of gleaming polished wood darker than mahogany. A wide gravel road led straight to the entrance. Amelia parked, shut off the engine, got out of the car. The absence of a road branching around the house indicated that there was a private access road in back. Well, why not? Privilege was privilege.

She was bang on time. In fact, a clock somewhere inside was chiming as she raised her hand to ring the bell. It was answered by a stocky gray-haired woman in gray sweats and lavender Reeboks (housekeeper? secretary? nurse?), who acknowledged her with a nod. The entrance hall was long and wide and paneled in bright, satiny wood, the only furnishings a handsome hammered brass umbrella stand and a long oak pew bench. No carpet on the parquet floor, and Amelia wondered about this until she remembered the wheelchair.

She was ushered into a room at the end of the hall, and that was where the carpets were. Not on the floor, on the walls—Navajo weavings of an age and antiquity seldom encountered outside museums. The room, large and almost square, with shuttered french windows at the far end, furnished with austere Spanish colonial pieces, made Amelia feel for a moment as if she had boarded a train for Versailles and wound up in Taos. Facing her, Henrietta Hazelton sat behind a refectory table of some blackish wood on the verge of petrification. Her shawl today was heathered banker's gray cashmere; her brooch looked like the same one she had worn at the memorial service. The Roman emperor's visage was as grim as Amelia remembered. At close range, her eyes were much lighter than they had appeared in the chapel, steely gray and very piercing.

"Thank you for seeing me, Mrs. Hazelton. Please forgive me for gawking. This room isn't at all what I anticipated."

"Which would, I imagine, be Chippendale and Queen Anne and a lot of bird's-eye maple. The rest of the house is traditional. I arranged this room to please myself. Now that we've disposed of the amenities, I trust that you will cut to the chase, as they say. Before you do, I should inform you that I agreed to see you because people whose judgment I respect do not believe you wrote those letters. Please do not interpret that as a vote of confidence."

"I don't. I'm beyond the point where that would matter. I'm going to regret having opened my mouth as long as I live—nothing's going to change that. But I didn't come here to dump on you, I came here to try to find out what made Katherine Ellsworth tick. She struck me as a very self-contained woman with plenty of grit. The last time I saw her, she made it clear that she'd heard all about my five minutes of fame, and it seemed to amuse her. Of course a lot changes when the hypothetical becomes real and strikes home, but still—I'm aware of what Katherine had on her conscience. I suppose you're wondering how, but—"

"Never mind how, Mrs. Cunningham. Just get on with it."

"Well, I just can't see her secret as all that devastating. I mean, she borrowed money—illicitly, I'll grant—but she intended to replace it and in fact did replace it. So somebody found out and threatened to spill the beans. So what? I can't see her getting all bent out of shape about what people she didn't care about thought of her."

Henrietta Hazelton gripped the arms of her wheelchair with white-knuckled fingers. "It seems to have escaped you that it was a question of honor."

"Perhaps. If you define honor as scouts and schoolgirls do. Did Katherine? And if she did, wasn't she the sort to stand up and admit to wrongdoing? On the other hand—What I'm about to suggest is likely to make you jump down my throat. I've heard—It seems to be common knowledge that Katherine's marriage wasn't the happiest, that William wasn't faithful to her and—Well, suppose what she feared might come out was some scandal about *him*. Say an involvement with a girl who was underage or—I don't know. I'm merely speculating."

"You certainly are." The gray eyes were frosted over; the anger in Henrietta Hazelton's voice was barely under control. "Precisely what do you expect from me, Mrs. Cunningham? Surely not confirmation of whatever salacious gossip you've been listening to?"

"No. Not really. I merely wondered if the prospect of seeing William's sins publicized might have driven her over the edge, that's all."

"And I wonder why you are wondering, Mrs. Cunningham. Katherine's suicide was an act of desperation. The motivation has not been questioned by anyone else. I fail to comprehend why you should refuse to accept it. What conceivable difference could it make to you?"

"None, I suppose, but—Well, it surprises me that Katherine should have been targeted rather than William. Doesn't it surprise you? Just a little?"

"Nothing in this life surprises me anymore." Henrietta Hazelton wheeled a 180-degree turn and presented Amelia with her back.

I've blown it, Amelia thought. But was there any way not to have blown it? Was there any way to get Henrietta Hazelton to voice an opinion as to whether Katherine Ellsworth might have committed suicide because of her husband's disgrace rather than her own? Still, the question had to be asked.

If Henrietta Hazelton jibbed at that one, how would she react to the next? For a moment, Amelia was tempted to back off, run not walk to the nearest exit.

No. She had to see it through. She had known this wasn't going to be any day at the beach before she came.

"The thing the whole premise hinges on—I realize this is going to sound like the ultimate in effrontery, but—Was Katherine in the habit of opening her husband's mail?"

Henrietta Hazelton didn't reply. She didn't have to: her rigid shoulders expressed outrage.

And that was that. Amelia wasn't surprised. She had come here on a fool's errand. Too bad she hadn't known that in advance.

But she had known in advance. Almost known, anyway. And still she had come. And if she had it to do over again would do the same.

Henrietta Hazelton wheeled her chair around slowly, to fix Amelia with eyes as brilliant—and cold—as the diamonds in her brooch.

"If you'll excuse me, Mrs. Cunningham, it's been a long day and I'm rather tired. I can't see anything to be gained by prolonging this conversation."

"No, I suppose not. I appreciate that this must have been painful for you. I'm sorry. The things I tried to find out from you are the sort of things it isn't polite to ask about, but I had to ask, even at the risk of coming on like a guilt-ridden ghoul. Good-bye, Mrs. Hazelton. Thank you for your time."

Walking out of the room, Amelia was acutely aware of her lug rubber soles squeaking on the parquet floor. The hall seemed twice as long as before. There was no sign of the woman in the lavender Reeboks, and Amelia had to let herself out. She felt small and abject, like a child sent to bed without supper. She needed all her self-control not to make a mad dash for the car, and, once she was in it, not to tear away as if the state police were after her. At the end of the driveway she bore left, away from Northvale, toward nowhere in particular. Maybe she could ride off her chagrin.

Well, she'd asked for it, hadn't she? Sure. But asking for it didn't make getting it any easier to take.

So okay. Her million-to-one long shot hadn't come home. Now what? Where did she go from here?

Nowhere—the only sensible answer. Finding out whether Katherine Ellsworth had opened a letter addressed to her husband was clearly impossible. If what Suzanne had said about William Ellsworth was true, then Katherine had had ample cause for jealousy, and jealous wives are known to spy on their husbands. Katherine might have opened her husband's mail routinely.

Might have. Maybe. Only a possibility. Even if Henrietta Hazelton had opened up and contributed some sort of validation, it was still only a possibility. No way of actually knowing.

Grant, for the sake of argument, that Katherine had opened the anonymous letter. Why then would she kill herself? Because her husband's repeated infidelities had driven her to the brink and the threat to go public with something more than garden-variety adultery sent her over? Somehow that didn't sound like Katherine Ellsworth.

Amelia sighed. Who was she to say what sounded like Katherine Ellsworth and what didn't? She had barely known Katherine Ellsworth.

Suzanne was convinced it was murder, not suicide.

Suzanne's was hardly an objective opinion.

But that didn't necessarily mean Suzanne was wrong.

Face it. No amount of speculation would get her farther than that. Short of enlisting a medium to make contact with the next world, she would never know whether or not William Ellsworth had killed his wife. And if she did know he was a murderer, what then? What could she possibly do about it? Shout it from the rooftops? Demented idea.

What she had to do now was what everyone had been urging her to do all along, put the whole thing behind her.

How?

Amelia passed a sign informing her that the ferry for New York was straight ahead, and realized that she was miles and miles from home. Great. Now she had conspicuous gas consumption to add to her sins. Next time, she vowed as she made a U-turn that couldn't possibly be legal, she would do her ruminating on foot.

Gas wasn't the only thing she had wasted. It was getting on for seven o'clock, and she had left a note for Gabriel saying she would be home around six. He might be wondering at not finding her. He might even be a little ticked off. Not that he expected her to stick to a schedule—any more than she expected it of him—but they were always scrupulous about keeping each other informed of their whereabouts. He would certainly be wondering about dinner, which she always had ready at eight, give or take a few minutes or so.

She didn't quite burn rubber heading home, but it was only seven-twenty when she turned into the driveway. The house was dark, and inside she found her note to Gabriel exactly where she had left it. So he was late, too. No doubt he had tried to telephone. She went to check the answering machine. Uselessly—she had forgotten to switch it on.

Straightaway Amelia set to work on dinner, which was a sort of Irish stew, prepared yesterday—all she had to do was remove the crust of congealed lamb fat and set the pot on the stove to simmer. Just about Gabriel's favorite dish, or at least the one he cited as the primary reason for not turning vegetarian. *Crudités* with a sour cream/chive dip to begin, a salad of watercress and chicory to follow, Terry Tracy's cinnamon-laden apple flan to finish.

Concentrating on her own concerns was going to be the name of the game from now on, Amelia promised herself. No more brooding over what she couldn't undo, no more poking her nose in what was none of her business. She had a life, damn it! From now on, home was going to be a place Gabriel liked coming to, just as it had been in the past. He had been getting in later and later recently, and God knows she couldn't blame him. Who would be eager to walk through the door to face Misery Mary?

Gabriel arrived home at a quarter to eight. He had, he said, got into a discussion with Alex Frayn about a plan for a visiting poets lecture series, and they had decided to finish it over drinks. He had tried to call, but got no response, human or mechanical.

Amelia laughed; confessed that she'd forgotten to turn on the answering machine again. "As a matter of fact, I was late myself. Got caught up in some research and lost track of the time."

She felt a twinge. It was the first time she could recall having resorted to editing truth with Gabriel. She vowed to herself that it would be the last.

9

My wife! my wife! what wife? I have no wife.
O insupportable! O heavy hour!
Methinks it should be now a huge eclipse
Of sun and moon, and that th' affrighted globe
Did yawn at alteration.

And Othello, apparently frightened by his own prediction, flung himself to the floor of the stage and curled up into fetal position.

I have no wife. . . . Methinks it should be now a huge eclipse of sun and moon. . . . I have no wife. . . . Methinks it should be now a huge eclipse of sun and moon. . . . I have no wife. . . . The words echoed and re-echoed in Amelia's head with an import Shakespeare never intended.

Othello was right. When a man kills his wife, the world should take notice. Not an eclipse, not an earthquake, but something. He shouldn't be allowed to get away with it. Or was it naive to believe in retribution? An abstract word for an abstract idea. The stuff of the printed page, the boards, the big and little screens. Not the stuff of the real world. People did get away with murder in the real world. Time and time again.

Here she was, back at the old stand. For days she had kept

herself too busy to think, and this evening's outing was supposed to be a distraction. *Distraction.*

Was William Ellsworth a murderer? Had he received the anonymous letter and seen a way to get rid of his wife and taken it? If so, why? From the way Suzanne talked, Katherine hadn't been any obstacle to his conquests.

Maybe William had simply grown tired of having a millstone round his neck. Maybe Katherine had blown all his assets on Canton porcelain. Maybe—

"For a minute there I was afraid Othello wasn't going to be able to unknot himself in time to get up and let your namesake in," Gabriel murmured in Amelia's ear.

She was suddenly aware that the play was over and everyone was applauding, including herself: amazing how the body could perform on automatic pilot.

"Dance training, most likely," she said, proving that the mind could perform on automatic pilot, too. For she hadn't consciously seen Othello get up. Or realize he'd been conned. Or stab himself. The close of the play had gone right past her.

The applause was prolonged, resounding through the Broadway-sized theater (the gift of a stagestruck Northvale alumna), necessitating three curtain calls. A response to the energy and enthusiasm of the cast of young professionals rather than to the success of the performance.

"I think it's commendable, mounting productions of Shakespeare and barnstorming around campuses," Alex Frayn said afterwards, when the two couples were in a restaurant for a late supper. A big, burly man, he had fuzzy red hair sprouting everywhere hair could sprout. "Good training for the actors and great for the students."

"Even if many of them come to avoid having to read the play," Gabriel said. "Or rather a synopsis and crib notes."

"The age we live in." Alex started combing his beard with all ten fingers. "But to be perfectly candid, it will be a long time before I'll be able to think of Desdemona singing 'Willow' with a straight face. God, with a voice like that the girl should have been advised to chant the lines, like Rex Harrison in *My Fair Lady.*"

"I thought it came off anyway," Betty Frayn said. She took

hold of her husband's wrists and lowered them gently to the table. "She was a little rough around the edges, but she might be a decent actress someday. She certainly looked right for the part. Actually, I thought the casting was first rate from the point of view of how the thing looked. And I especially liked Emilia being Japanese. You know, bred to obedience and serving the male and all that. It made for a lot of impact at the end, when she denounces Iago."

"I liked her being Japanese, too," Amelia said. "It made the business with the handkerchief convincing for once. I've always been bothered by how meekly Emilia turns it over to Iago—one would think she would at least wonder why he wants it."

"Exactly." Betty smiled warmly at Amelia. A rare occurrence. Betty, barely five feet tall, with blue eyes and hair like lemon candy floss, Goldilocks to Alex's Papa Bear, was a gourmet cook and pluperfect housewife; around her Amelia always felt (or was made to feel) that she didn't come up to scratch.

The food arrived, demanding attention and putting an end to the discussion of the play before Gabriel or Alex could jump in with an objection to racial stereotypes. The restaurant was new, superceding a Mexican cantina that had not caught on (a patron claimed to have found a strip of cardboard in her enchilada), and vegetarian, boasting a cuisine based on Vermont produce and dairy products. Gabriel, Alex, and Betty had chosen the feature of the day, Curried Three Sisters Chowder. In Amelia's mind, the name conjured up visions of snow-laden steppes, though she knew that the Three Sisters were the spirits of corn and squash and beans, guardians of the crops in Iroquois mythology, and had nothing to do with Chekhov. Her choice was mushroom bisque, and she didn't regret it (however much it tasted like Campbell's Cream of Mushroom soup with a lot of rubbery mushrooms added), because the smell of the curry wafting her way made her eyes water. As usual, Betty launched into a detailed critique of what she was eating and, as usual, Amelia tuned her out.

But tuning out Betty meant opening the channel to other things. Unwelcome things. Things Amelia had almost managed to suppress until *Othello* churned them up again.

Was William Ellsworth a murderer?

She would never know.

How could she bear not knowing?

"Amelia." Gabriel poked her in the ribs.

"What? Oh, I'm sorry. I was woolgathering."

"Obviously. Betty asked if she could sample your bread."

"Of course." Amelia felt herself blushing as she held out the plate of what looked like stone-ground wheat bread. "Have as much as you like. I've finished my soup." Belatedly, Amelia realized that she should have offered Betty a taste.

"Thanks, but a bite will do." Betty smiled (perfunctory—not the genuine article she had flashed earlier), cut off a small wedge of Amelia's bread, buttered it deftly, popped it into her mouth, chewed. Silence at the table as the verdict was awaited. "Delicious. Made with tahini. The entrées here might not be world beaters, but the breads are first rate." She passed the plate back to Amelia. "Eat it. I'm too full of cornbread."

Amelia didn't really want any bread, but she broke off a piece and buttered it and ate it. Delicious, of course. Betty was always right about food. Amelia found herself wishing, not for the first time, that Alex Frayn wasn't Gabriel's best buddy in the English department. Luckily, it wasn't a condition of their friendship that their wives should get along. But then, why should it have been? She and Suzanne had always got on like a house afire, yet Gabriel had never had much time for Hal Longman, who was totally lacking in small talk and was given to long silences that induced self-consciousness in chatterers.

There was sufficient bread and butter on Amelia's plate to see her through coffee, so she passed on dessert. The others plumped for maple walnut cheesecake, a house specialty for which, the menu proclaimed, Vermonters traveled for miles. "They might just as well have stayed at home," Betty pronounced, and the men didn't disagree, though they finished their cheesecake down to the last crumb.

On the drive home, Gabriel remarked that he hoped Amelia had enjoyed herself wherever she had spent the evening "because it sure as hell wasn't with *Othello.*"

For the second time within the hour, Amelia felt the heat of mortification rising to her face. Only this time it was worse. Far,

far worse. She almost wished she had Othello's option of curling up to make things go away, at least for a little while. She didn't. They wouldn't. Haltingly, she admitted that she had indeed been miles away (how could she deny it?) and apologized, hoping Gabriel would be satisfied with that.

He wasn't. His stiffness and his silence meant resentment. He wasn't going to ask, of course.

But what if he did? What would she say if he did?

Oh God. Welling up in her was an overpowering desire to tell him everything. Share her suspicion that William Ellsworth might be a murderer. Unload. Dump on him. If only she could.

She couldn't. Betraying Suzanne was unthinkable. Even if she could get past that, how could she burden Gabriel with such a hideous suspicion? William Ellsworth wasn't merely the head of the English department, he was almost worshiped by many of his younger colleagues. Hadn't Alex Frayn named his younger son William? And how many times had Gabriel trotted out the latest Ellsworth sayings and doings for her admiration?

Still, she had to say something to defuse the situation now.

Inspiration struck. "I'm ashamed to say that I wasn't in this world, I was in the next one, communing with dead celebrities. Trying to figure out ways to translate their messages into English that won't make people split their sides laughing."

It worked. Gabriel's resentment dissolved in hearty laughter as, for the remainder of the ride, she regaled him with some of the messages from the manuscript she was editing. The evening ended in uproarious merriment (how long since they had laughed together?). Inevitably, one thing led to another, and another.

Only later, after Gabriel had fallen asleep, did Amelia reflect that the successful and most satisfying denouement had come about as the result of deception. It had been easy, so easy it scared her a little. Was a talent for deception one she really wanted to cultivate?

10

Amazing, isn't it, that people are still writing books about me more than fifty years after the *Itasca* lost contact with my plane and I vanished into thin air? They come up with no end of theories. Some say I wound up in the briny because of engine failure or running out of petrol or navigational error (though all those reports of Fred Noonan's drinking have nothing to do with it—he was sober when we left Lac and there wasn't a drop on board, I promise you). Others say I landed on Mile Atoll and Fred and I were captured by the Japanese and taken to Saipan and executed as spies. Well, I can't blame people for speculating, especially since what really happened was more astonishing than their wildest flights of fancy.

It's quite true that we were somewhat off course when we lost radio contact, but I could have corrected that and brought the Electra down at Howland with the supply of petrol on board, low though it was, had not Fred suffered some sort of seizure and passed out. I had to fly blind, and it was hopeless. I had just about decided to touch down in the middle of the ocean and hope for rescue before we died of exposure when I spotted land directly ahead. I cleared some palms and touched down on a beach. Fred was conscious but delirious and kept asking for water. I gave him what was left on board and went to find more. I had to walk quite a distance before I found a stream, and I was away from the plane for some time. When I got back, Fred had disappeared. I noticed footsteps in the sand leading down to the water. The poor chap must have wandered off in his delirium and drowned. Well, it was terribly sad-making. I thought about his poor wife and cried for a bit. Then I pulled up my socks and tried to send an SOS, but the radio wouldn't work, probably because sand had got into it. So there I was, on my ownio. I decided to explore the island or whatever it was, and here's where the astonishing part begins. . . .

Amelia groaned aloud, stopped reading the postmortal words of Amelia Earhart, and pushed the manuscript away from her. A break was in order. Or a drink, if it weren't too early in the day for that. Something, anyway, to help her face whatever was coming next. A potpourri of *Robinson Crusoe, Lost Horizon,* and *A Handful of Dust?* Perhaps a straightforward account of a visit to the lost continent of Atlantis? However idiotic the substance, Amelia's editorial offices would be limited to tightening and changing the English suburban accents of the author to those of someone from Kansas. Never mind that she knew full well that Earhart's final flight had, in the view of many, been a mission of folly; that Howland Island, small and poorly charted, had been easier to miss than to find, even by an experienced and cold sober navigator; that Earhart had never taken the time to master the radio or learn Morse; that back in the pioneer days of aviation a staggering number of pilots took off into the wild blue yonder and were never heard from again. No, any or all of the above wouldn't do for this author. The navigator had to have a seizure. And of course there would have to be Shangri-la or whatever instead of a watery grave for Earhart.

Amelia got up from her chair and stretched. God help her if

her mother, who had named her after Earhart, ever found out about her part in disseminating this fairy tale—she would never hear the end of it. Fortunately, it wouldn't be the sort of book her mother was likely to read. Still, with her mother's nose for ferreting out every word that had ever been written about Earhart—

Don't think about that. Thinking about the manuscript was bad enough. Maybe if she played hookey for a while, got out of the house to recharge her batteries, she could face sorting out Earhart's beyond-the-grave utterances with more enthusiasm. No. Enthusiasm wasn't really the word. Tolerance? Equanimity? Patience? Any of those seemed too positive.

Outside, the day was beautiful, the kind of day that made you believe spring might truly be on the way. Amelia decided to drive to the Northvale campus, leave her car in the parking lot, and trek over the hill behind the skating rink and down over a little dale to the woods beyond. Nobody was likely to be there. She would pack an apple and cheese and crackers and fill a Thermos with bouillon and wander in solitude. Who knew? Maybe out in the open the spirit of Amelia Earhart would send *her* a message. Why should that hair-brained Englishwoman have a monopoly on communion with the departed?

As she passed the college library, she decided to stop in for a quick look at what was available among the recent acquisitions and trolleys of the to-be-shelved returned books, and lucked out with both volumes of the Arthur Cash biography of Laurence Sterne. She took them to the car, concealed them under a sweater, and locked the car. Overdoing the security, probably. Nobody wanted to rip off books. Last year Hal Longman's Jeep Cherokee had been stolen from the campus, and the books inside it had been dumped on Route 7 and duly returned to him (the Cherokee had never been heard of again). Walking away from the car, Amelia came face-to-face with a couple of Gabriel's students who had been to the house at an end-of-term party last spring, and the greeting they gave her was friendly and unforced and unembarrassed. Was it possible they hadn't heard? No—the student grapevine was second to none. More likely the entire episode was old news to them, part of the historical record. Hardly a thought to upgrade one's estimation of human nature, especially a stone's throw from the chapel where the memorial service for Katherine Ellsworth had been held.

Amelia followed the paved campus path to its end, a small plaza framed by sentinel elms fronting a concrete bunker of a building, the skating rink that was the home of the Northvale Otters, the college hockey team. In the center of the plaza was a bronze statue of Mercury, wearing helmet and what looked like long johns and ice skates with blades that left considerable space between his feet and the pedestal (a romantic post office in the days when lovers wrote letters to one another instead of picking up the phone). She went past the skating rink to the steep hill in back, known since time immemorial as Brangaene, because a lookout stationed at the top could issue a warning to lovers in the woods on the other side. Nowadays, when anybody could do practically anything on campus, trysts in the woods were pretty much obsolete, and Amelia sometimes wondered whether any of the current crop of students, other than a few music majors, knew how the hill had got its name. Or cared.

The climb was steep. Mounting briskly, Amelia was slightly winded when she reached the top. The descent was gentler, and she took it slowly, then speeded up again to cross the barren brown field to the trees. Last time she had been here, after the first snowfall of the season, snow had coated the ground and frosted the branches of the trees. The ground was moist and loamy now, the unburdened branches looked strong and full of vigor, and the air smelled fresh, rich, and slightly gamy. There wasn't a soul in sight. It never failed to amaze her that, outside of foliage season, when tourists flocked to every available tree, she had these woods to herself. Perhaps the amorous associations of the past put people off. She didn't know and didn't want to know. From the start this had been her favorite spot in all of Northvale, a refuge from college politics, town versus gown, Vermonters versus flatlanders, the whole social hurly-burly. Of late she had avoided coming here for fear of polluting the atmosphere with her overload of angst. Perhaps silly, perhaps not. Now that she was on the way toward getting out from under, that was no longer a major concern.

The earth squished a little underfoot as she walked. There was no danger of getting lost, even when the footpaths were buried under snow. Long ago, arrows had been gouged into the trunks of trees bordering the paths. Environmental purists still made an issue of that, though what they hoped their protests would achieve at this late date Amelia couldn't begin to guess. Removal of the desecrated trees? Coverage of the desecration with fig leaves? An ordinance to prevent others in future doing likewise? For her part, city born and bred, she was glad the arrows were there. It wasn't the first time she had found herself at odds with hard-line environmentalists. Mostly the conflict had to do with jewelry or *objets d'art*. If she came upon a beautiful piece of old ivory or tortoise shell worked as only craftsmen of bygone days could have worked it, she felt that, since the elephant or the turtle hadn't died for her, buying the piece was okay. But perhaps that was a rationalization.

Well, she wasn't going to add worry about the planet to her other burdens. She had come out for a holiday, damn it!

She walked aimlessly, giving her senses free rein. Letting her mind shut down. How long she rambled she had no idea, until her stomach growled to tell her it was time for lunch. She took a big black plastic garbage bag out of her purse, unfolded it, and spread it under a tree. An act that made her feel like the sort of person designer toilet-seat covers were marketed for, but she had learned the hard way how damp the ground could be. The cheese she had brought was Jarlsberg, the apple was tart and green. She cut slices of each with her bone-handled pocketknife, stacked the slices on sesame-seed wafers, and munched contentedly.

She had finished eating and was opening the Thermos when she heard a woman's cry of passion somewhere in the trees behind her. At least that was what it sounded like. She set the Thermos down on the ground and sat absolutely still, suddenly feeling as if she were eavesdropping in somebody's boudoir.

She had an impulse to pack up and clear out. She resisted it. Ridiculous to feel that she was spying. She had every right to be here. For all she knew, there was nothing to spy on. Maybe what she had heard wasn't what she thought it was. Maybe it was the cry of an animal in distress. Or some kind of birdcall. What did she know about birds?

She continued to sit perfectly still, listening intently. The sound, whatever it might have been, was not repeated. She heard nothing that could have been construed as people noises. Or animal noises. Or bird noises.

She opened the Thermos and poured bouillon into the cup. She would drink up and go home. Back to the mythical adventures of Amelia Earhart. With any luck, she would be better able to cope now. Well, marginally better able to cope. If things got too bad, she could always resort to an early martini. Not her usual crutch, but what the hell. And, naturally, only if things got really, really—

Footsteps. Unmistakably human footsteps. Heavy shoes squelching the earth somewhere behind her. She shrank back against the tree, trying to make herself invisible. Why hadn't she gone when the going was good?

The footsteps came closer, a little behind her and definitely to her left. A good chance whoever it was would pass by without seeing her. She held her breath.

A man came into view about five feet to her left, walking briskly but not hurrying. If he turned his head, there was no way he could miss spotting her. He didn't turn his head. He kept on walking and was soon lost from sight.

Not soon enough. No mistaking that silver thatch of hair, that patrician profile. He was William Ellsworth.

Amelia let out her breath. Her stomach flip-flopped, and for a moment she feared her lunch might come up on her. The moment passed. With a flutter, her stomach settled back to normal. Gone was any thought of leaving—wild horses couldn't have dragged her away before she set eyes on William Ellsworth's paramour.

She didn't have long to wait before she heard once again the tread of heavily shod feet. The girl came out of the trees in the same place William Ellsworth had appeared. Amelia recognized her. A student. A tall, slim girl, very noticeable on campus because of a magnificent mane of fiery red hair and because she always wore jodhpurs and riding boots. The jodhpurs weren't visible today, hidden by a long olive green canvas outback coat. Like William Ellsworth, the girl didn't turn her head, just kept on going. The last sight of her was the twitch of an olive green coat-tail. And Amelia thought: what great protection that coat must be from the wet ground. Much better than carrying garbage bags around.

Terrific. Just what God gave her a brain for, to come up with insights like that. Next she would be thinking about acquiring an outback coat for future visits to the woods.

Future visits to the woods. Amelia shuddered. She wouldn't be coming back here anytime soon, that was for sure. Her private retreat, hidey-hole, whatever, wasn't hers anymore. Right now she wanted to get up and run as far away as she could as fast as she could.

Her body wouldn't move. It might have been made of lead.

The bastard. The self-centered, self-indulgent bastard. Poor Katherine wasn't even cold in her grave.

God. Talk about freaking out. First fashion notes, then conventional platitudes. How idiotic could you get?

The bastard. The *bastard.*

Amelia was astonished by the force of her indignation. Was she to conclude that she had a wide, hitherto unsuspected streak of Mrs. Grundy in her makeup?

No. Not really. It was one thing to be told that William Ellsworth was a randy old buck, quite another to be confronted with the proof. Not that she had doubted Suzanne. Well, maybe she had. Maybe part of her was still holding fast to denial. But was it any wonder? Letting go would mean believing heart and soul in everything Suzanne had said.

Everything? That didn't necessarily follow. Just because William Ellsworth had an overdeveloped libido didn't mean he was a murderer. If he were, wouldn't he be more circumspect now?

Not if he was sure he had got away with it.

Round and round and round. Her mind was back on the all too familiar track.

Amelia closed her Thermos and stuffed it in her purse. She got to her feet, stooped and picked up the plastic garbage bag, folded it neatly, put it into a plastic carrier bag along with the relics of her lunch, stuffed the carrier bag in her purse. No sign that she had ever been here.

Shit. Why was she the one to worry about covering her tracks? *She* wasn't a criminal.

Less and less was "It's none of my business" a viable argument. If William Ellsworth had murdered his wife, it *was* her business, it was everybody's business.

If he had murdered his wife. Such a big, big "if."

11

The conclusion of the Earhart narrative as relayed by the English spiritualist was pretty much the sort of romantic folderol Amelia expected. The island where the Electra put down was totally unknown, inhabited by beautiful pale brown beings, unlettered but untainted by the vices of civilization and oh so wise. Earhart had contracted a fever that immobilized her for months; had fallen in love with her shaman/physician; had responded to the call of duty and tried to return to civilization and got as far as Sydney, where she happened to see a newspaper account of her husband's remarriage and— Any Hollywood hack of the thirties or forties could have drafted the scenario. About the content Amelia couldn't do anything but groan. As for the style, it took two full days and the better part of a morning to get rid of the English grace notes and find a voice that would inspire some degree of trust.

She was debating whether to go on to Steve McQueen or treat herself to a prelunch martini (hell, she had earned it) when the telephone rang. She thought about letting the machine answer but reached for the receiver instead.

"Hello."

"Mrs. Cunningham?" An imperious contralto, vaguely familiar.

"Yes."

"Henrietta Hazelton here. It's imperative that I speak with you. Could you come to see me? Directly, if possible."

"Well, I—" The hesitation stretched out to silence as Amelia, recalling the mortification of that first visit, groped for a polite way to refuse.

"I realize that this request can have little appeal. When you came to see me before, I found what you had to say repugnant and altogether unacceptable, and of course I made no secret of the fact. However, you gave me much to think about. I sincerely regret my intransigence and I hope you are willing to overlook it."

The tone was still imperious; the import was not. Amelia couldn't say no, though she would have liked to. It no longer seemed so important to hear what Henrietta Hazelton might have to say because the idea that William Ellsworth had murdered his wife no longer seemed so inconceivable. Amelia was almost used to it.

How long before she got used to the idea that he was going to get away with it?

Once again Amelia was admitted by the gray-haired woman in the lavender Reeboks and led through the long wood-paneled hall to the large room with the Spanish colonial furniture and the Navajo wall hangings. The curtains over the french windows were open, offering a view of a topiary garden. Once again Henrietta Hazelton was seated behind the dark refectory table; the diamond brooch today fastened a cashmere shawl the color of old ivory.

"Thank you for coming, Mrs. Cunningham. I take it as a favor, since I am reasonably certain that you had a more pleasant agenda for your afternoon. Please sit down."

Amelia hesitated, taken aback slightly by an invitation so conspicuously absent last time. The chairs in the room were primitive, slabs of dark wood on rough-hewn legs. Sitting down in the one nearest the table put her about eight feet away from Henrietta Hazelton, which didn't seem far enough.

"Perhaps it may expedite matters to say that although I tried to close my ears and my mind to you, Mrs. Cunningham, I heard you nonetheless. Everything you said forced me to the conclusion that the anonymous letter must have been sent to William, not Katherine."

"I advanced it as a hypothesis, not a certainty."

A regal wave of the hand dismissed this as a cavil. "You wouldn't have come to see me unless you were sure. There are only two ways you could be sure—either you sent the letters yourself, or you know who did and of course will not tell me. But by all means let us call it a hypothesis. If it's a valid one, then Katherine did not take her life for the reason everyone believes. We can rule out the possibility that she opened her husband's letter by mistake, since the letters sent to men were addressed 'Esquire.' "

Amelia opened her lips, closed them without voicing the "How do *you* know?" that would have been the logical question. People like Henrietta Hazelton never had any trouble finding out whatever they wanted to know.

"Therefore, the only reason Katherine might have taken her life is that she found the prospect of having some nasty little secret of William's exposed unendurable. Once I opened my mind to the idea, I began to understand why you felt you had to talk to me. What I couldn't quite see was why Katherine's motive should have mattered to you. Then I began to entertain the possibility that Katherine did not take her own life, and I finally realized what was behind the questions I wrongly attributed to prurient curiosity. You were trying to find out whether I thought William Ellsworth might be capable of murder. Am I correct?"

"Yes." Amelia sighed. "I was trying to ask the unaskable."

"Indeed you were. I give you full marks for courage. I asked you here today because I feel I owe you total honesty, in part to compensate for the reception I gave you last time. Unfortunately, the unaskable is also the unanswerable. Or rather, any answer I might give you would be very little use to you. If I told you that William Ellsworth has the murderer's thumb, or that his grandmother was a cousin of Lizzie Borden, would you be any further along?"

"Not really."

A faint smile twitched the corners of Henrietta Hazelton's stern mouth. "Actually, it was *my* grandmother who was Lizzie Borden's cousin. A distant one, I'm happy to say." The smile vanished. "My opinion, for whatever it might be worth to you, is that William Ellsworth is indeed capable of murder. That man is capable of any action he thinks would benefit him in any way, not excluding murder. Does that surprise you?"

"No, no. It's just that—" Amelia stopped. She couldn't very well say that the Brahmin style of call-'em-like-you-see-'em never failed to floor her. "I suppose I was still clinging to a faint hope that you would assure me the idea is unthinkable."

"Would you have believed me?"

"Probably not."

The shadow of a smile appeared again, disappeared again. "What I am about to say goes against the grain—I have always regarded the talebearer as the lowest form of sentient being. However, you sought my opinion and you shall have it. If William Ellsworth did indeed murder Katherine, it would have been merely a ceremonial finish. In every sense that matters, he murdered Katherine long ago. Trashed the passion she lavished on him. Broke her spirit. Deadened her mind. Turned her into the vestige of a woman that was all anybody who encountered her in recent years knew of her. I imagine you thought that I exaggerated her accomplishments at the memorial service, as one does on such occasions. I did not. I didn't have to. Her stature as a gardener was beyond dispute, and Northvale owes her more for services to the community than the selectmen have ever been willing to admit. All that was very fine, but it was by no means the best of her. The best of her was the girl I went to school with.

"I wish you could have known her as I did, Mrs. Cunningham. You would have liked her. She was bright. Articulate. Above all, ardent—always seeking a cause worthy of that ardor. Unfortunately, she didn't find a cause, she found William Ellsworth. On the surface, a wonderful catch. Looks. Brains. Charm. Impeccable lineage—not quite the *Mayflower,* but not far behind. Everything a girl could ask for except money. Katherine fell madly in love with him. Believed that in serving as William's helpmeet she had found her destiny. It's always a mistake, I think, trying to fulfill oneself through another person. Don't you agree?"

"Oh yes. But it's only in recent years that women have started thinking that way." Amelia felt herself blushing. "I mean—"

"You mean you didn't expect to hear that from someone who grew up in the Dark Ages. No, don't bother to protest—I'm not offended. You're quite right, actually. For my generation it was the norm, though one wonders what all those angels in the house might have said about their lives, had anyone asked. Never mind. The point at issue here isn't whether a woman's self-immolation is ever justified, it's whether William Ellsworth was worthy of Katherine's. He wasn't. In her he found someone he could lean on, and lean he did. She was his prop, his anchor, his support. Without her, he couldn't have summoned the willpower or the application or the gumption to push through the academic jungle, and he was wise enough to realize that. Oh, perhaps he wasn't as calculating as I make him sound. Perhaps he loved her, insofar as so shallow a vessel can love. He betrayed her almost from the start, of course. The first time she found out he was unfaithful, she was desolated. Confronted him and got a confession, an apology, a promise never to do it again—the gamut of remorse. He did do it again, needless to say. Again and again and again. Eventually, she stopped protesting. Grew the carapace that all of us were only too familiar with. Literally cultivated her garden and gave the leftover feeling and intelligence to whatever was at hand. Which was Northvale's gain, I suppose." The tone was bitter.

"I'm sorry," Amelia said. Automatically. Inadequately.

The gray eyes looked as hard as the diamonds in the brooch. "That is all I am able to offer you, Mrs. Cunningham. It hardly rises above the level of gossip. Certainly I cannot be accused of objectivity."

"No." All at once Amelia found herself wondering what William Ellsworth's side of the story would sound like. Surely it was a possibility that Katherine, like so many women of her generation (like so many women of the present generation, for that matter), had poured everything into a relationship instead of taking control of her own life, and William, like all too many men, had found the burden intolerable.

Simplistic. And anyway, what did it matter whether William had a side of the story to tell if he had murdered his wife?

Had he murdered his wife?

102

"A penny for them." Henrietta Hazelton's face was less stony; the gray stare had softened considerably.

Amelia sighed. "Nothing very profound, I'm afraid. My mind balks at the same thing it's balked at all along. Why? From everything I've heard—and everything you say confirms it—William Ellsworth's life has been pretty much the way he wanted it for quite some time. Katherine didn't really cramp his style. Why should he want to kill her? Unless there's something involved I don't know about. Money, for instance."

Henrietta Hazelton shook her head. "Katherine had a small trust fund that reverts to a cousin. Her life insurance carried a provision against suicide benefits—I checked. A financial motive seems highly unlikely."

"Then why? I can't even begin to imagine a motive."

"Nor can I. But who can say what constitutes a motive for murder except the murderer?"

"You're right, I suppose." Exactly what Suzanne had said.

"Whether I am or not scarcely signifies. Legally, motive counts for little except impressing juries. What counts is evidence, and in this instance there is none and no hope of obtaining any. I wish there were. Believe me, I wish there were. I cannot begin to tell you how much it means to be able to say that to someone, Mrs. Cunningham. To *share*—I trust that's the correct buzzword. I sincerely hope hearing it is some recompense for your journey here."

"Well, after talking to you I don't feel quite so much as if I'm shouting to myself in a closet. Thank you, Mrs. Hazelton."

"It's I who should be thanking you. For giving me back the Katherine I knew. A part of her, at least. The best part died long ago."

"I'm sorry." Again it sounded inadequate.

"I know you are. Try not to be so hard on yourself, my dear. You are not responsible for Katherine's fate, only perhaps for giving it a slight push. The seeds of her destruction were sown long before you ever came upon the scene. It's not the first time I've had cause to think that more harm is done in this world by love than by any other passion."

"That's harsh."

"Is it? Perhaps. Nonetheless, I'm thankful I was spared. I

genuinely liked my husband. I respected him. Since he died, I feel the loss of his companionship keenly. That's about all. Anytime I start wondering whether I might have missed something, the thought of Katherine brings me to my senses."

Amelia felt a stab of pity for the granite-faced, arrogant woman in the wheelchair. Bereft of companionship, bereft of the friendship that had clearly meant so much to her. Bereft, whatever she might say, of the tender memories that were supposed to provide solace for age and a diminished life. Or was that sentimentality?

How would Henrietta Hazelton react to pity? Laugh it to scorn, most likely.

But who knew? Who knew anything anymore?

12

Tonight Millicent Neumeyer wore hand-dyed silk in the blue/violet arc of the spectrum, yards and yards of it draped around her ample six-foot frame like a toga, and above it her freshly waved and blue-rinsed head overlooked most of the crowd. A very large crowd, as befitted the president's spring-term inaugural bash. The atmosphere was genuinely festive. If spring term was beginning, could summer vacation be far behind?

Amelia looked around the vast mahogany-paneled ballroom with the myriad windows (amazing how regal it looked when the plum velvet curtains were closed) and discovered, somewhat to her surprise, that the trepidation she had been feeling all day was gone. Because Millicent had made a point of complimenting her on her appearance?

" 'She was a vision of delight when now she gleamed upon my sight.' Or some such thing. It's not my period, naturally."

The words were spoken in a quavering high tenor behind Amelia's back. She turned and saw, with no surprise, Eliot Parking, Northvale's brilliant associate professor of modern literature. He wore a gold silk shirt with a large jabot and billowing sleeves, tight black velvet pants, and gold-embroidered black kid desert boots. His sculptured curls, bronze the last time Amelia had seen him, were pure gold tonight.

"Hello, Eliot. You look dazzling."

"Don't I always? But it's you who deserve the kudos tonight. Paisley is definitely *you,* dear. Especially gray paisley—marvelous with your hair. A Liberty wool challis, isn't it?"

"Yes. I picked it up in London ages ago. For years my sister has been begging me to let her do something with it, and I finally decided to let her."

"She did the right thing. Obviously." He waved an admonishing finger in front of Amelia's face. "Naughty, naughty, naughty, stealing the spotlight from me. But I'm willing to forgive you, provided that you don't make a habit of it."

Eliot bent forward for the obligatory cheek kissing, almost drowning Amelia in Mitsouko, a perfume that brought back childhood memories of an adored aunt, and floated away.

A compliment on one's appearance from Eliot Parking, however backhanded (and never mind the deliberate misquotation of Wordsworth), was nothing to sneeze at, and Amelia felt her spirits rising. She looked around for Gabriel, who had gone to load up at the buffet table, and spotted him fifteen feet away, both hands full, temporarily derailed by Otto Strassman, guest professor in the English department, renowned eighteenth-century scholar, and crashing bore. Poor Gabriel. She turned, and spotted Suzanne Longman coming her way.

"How goes it, kemosabay?" Suzanne said. "I must say you're looking a damn sight better than you did the last time I saw you."

It was Amelia's first confrontation with Suzanne since that never-to-be-forgotten conversation in Suzanne's kitchen. "I could say the same about you, only it wouldn't be doing you justice. I knew that dress couldn't miss." The dress, cognac silk velvet with a champagne lace collar, set off the russet coils of Suzanne's hair to perfection; they had unearthed it in a vintage clothing shop during a curio hunt they had made together last spring.

Last spring. Only a year ago, and it seemed like twenty. At least.

"Your dress isn't exactly chopped liver. Who knows? Maybe after enough time passes we'll be back to our old happy-go-lucky selves, a couple of fraus who think fashion statements matter." Suzanne brushed Amelia's cheek with icy lips and moved away.

Amelia watched her go, elegant and self-possessed as usual, giving nothing away. Watched her stop and exchange words with Gabriel, who had extricated himself from Otto Strassman and was approaching with food and drink.

"Sorry to be so long." Gabriel placed warm lips where Suzanne had placed cold ones. He held out a glass of white wine and a plate of hors d'oeuvres. "I got you some of everything."

"Good thinking."

"You look ravishing." He kissed her again, this time with a force that played a faint tune on her silver filigree pagoda earrings. "Best-dressed woman in the room. By far."

"You're hallucinating, but who am I to mind?" At that moment, Amelia felt on top of the world. Of course the high wouldn't last, that was too much to hope for, but maybe she could get through the evening before the inevitable downer. She took a sip of wine. Too sweet. Pity.

"I'm going to have to desert you again," Gabriel murmured in her ear. "Politicking. Unless you want to be a party to it?"

"God, no. Unless you need me."

"Not really." He took an almond-stuffed olive off her plate and popped it into his mouth, gave her shoulder a squeeze, and ambled away.

Amelia took another sip of wine and over the top of her glass sighted Pam Blair bearing down on her. Tonight Pam was a vision of something or other: leopard-spotted bodysuit that fitted her long, slim frame as if painted on; hair stretched to a degree reminiscent of Elsa Lanchester in *Bride of Frankenstein* and spangled with gold dust; gold hoops in her ears big enough to put a hand through, if not a foot.

"Cat piss," Pam said. "Don't drink too much of it. I see your spouse has bugged off rather than face me."

"Oh no, nothing like that. He had some circulating to do, that's all."

"A likely story."

Amelia laughed, not too comfortably—she thought it all too

probable that Pam was right. "It's the only one I've got. You give new meaning to 'dressed to kill,' Pam."

"That's the idea. Give everybody something to remember me by. I'm having a blast watching them all twitch and squirm and fall all over themselves to take evasive action. My only major disappointment was Old Lady Neumeyer—complete sangfroid there." Pam hesitated. "Actually, would you believe she actually had the grace to call me up and tell me she was sorry I was leaving? Sounded as if she meant it, too."

"I'm not surprised. I've learned it's a mistake to underestimate her."

"Yeah. On the other hand, most people you can't underestimate. Her call was the only one I got. Amazing how being let go turns you into a nonperson almost instantaneously."

Amelia winced. "I'm truly sorry, Pam. I know I should have—"

"Hey, that wasn't a dig. You gave me the news straight when the department was prepared to let me twist in the wind—I owe you for that. Anyhow, you wouldn't be human if you had any thoughts to spare for anybody else's troubles lately. For what it's worth, I never believed for a minute you wrote those letters. Not your style."

"Thanks." Amelia recalled her own suspicions of Pam and felt a twinge. Not much of a twinge. As her sins went these days, this one was almost negligible. "What's next for you? Or is that a tactless question?"

"Tactless as hell." Pam grinned widely. "The truth is, I'll be hitting the lecture circuit. With a contract that guarantees twice what Northvale College pays me. But I'd rather you didn't tell anybody yet."

"I won't," Amelia promised. God forbid she should deprive Pam of the pleasure of watching people twitch at the sight of her. "I couldn't be more glad for you."

"Yeah. I know." Pam stooped and kissed Amelia's cheek lightly. "See you around." She swaggered off, and people cleared a path for her, almost as though she were the jungle cat her bodysuit imitated.

Amelia tried hard to keep a straight face. Suddenly all her

amusement was wiped away as she caught sight of Samson Rigby, gazing at Pam with eyes full of hunger and longing. In a moment his eyes were back in neutral, but Amelia was sure enough of what she'd seen to realize that Gabriel had it all wrong: Sam Rigby wanted Pam out of Northvale because he coveted her, not her black literature course.

Passion. Lust. Sex all over the place. Jumping into her sight lines wherever she turned her eyes. It was enough to make her wonder whether she had been walking around blindfolded till now.

People closed ranks behind Pam, and movement revealed Gabriel across the room, talking animatedly to Alex Frayn. Amelia felt a pang of disappointment that Gabriel hadn't hung in there to face Pam. Foolish. Why should he have? Life had so many battles—one had to pick and choose.

"What I wouldn't give to overhear *that* conversation," said a voice in Amelia's ear. She turned and saw Betty Frayn beside her, wearing a cornflower blue dress with ruffles at the wrists and throat, pale hair fluffed out like floss. Betty's eyes were focused on Gabriel and Alex.

"Why?"

Betty shrugged. "Forewarned is forearmed, I guess. Against whatever deviltry they're hatching." She smiled with tight lips. "Just making small talk. You look wonderful, Amelia. Quite the most elegant woman in the room."

The tone was grudging, with a slight edge of sarcasm. Amelia chose to take the compliment at face value, expressed her thanks, and was relieved when Betty took herself off. Something had got Betty's back up, that much was clear. Something had prompted that dig at her husband and Gabriel. Why "deviltry" in a conversation between colleagues who also happened to be friends? Pique at being excluded? Possibly. Amelia recalled the wife of one of Gabriel's friends in graduate school, who once turned down a dinner invitation with, "My husband has to work on his idiot thesis." Maybe it was resentment of Alex's commitment to his work that was bugging Betty, maybe it was resentment of male bonding, maybe it was something else entirely. Who knew? Who cared? The truth was, Amelia was no more interested in what caused the cracks in the perfect little woman façade than she was in the façade itself.

Amelia caught Gabriel's eye. He smiled, detached himself from Alex Frayn, made his way toward her. Something fluttered in her chest, as always at the sight of him. It wasn't only partisanship that rated him the handsomest man in this crowd, most crowds. Tonight he had on the deep burgundy corduroy jacket with the pile so wide and deep it looked like velvet. Just right for his dark coloring; she was glad she had overridden his protest (mild) that it made him look like a Victorian impresario.

"Everybody tells me I'm keeping the best-looking company in the room," Gabriel said. He came very close and put his lips to her ear. "The wine is the absolute pits. Be careful."

"Now you tell me."

They both laughed. For the first time in ages, Amelia felt her life had regained some semblance of normality. Probably because everybody was so determinedly behaving as if that were so.

How quickly people forgot. Or pretended to.

None of that. Not now. Now was the moment to go with the flow, get whatever sustenance was to be got from all the waves of supportiveness.

"I've been told they're uncorking a case of drinkable chablis even as we speak," Gabriel said. "Now if we could just find a convenient potted palm—"

A woman's laughter resounded through the room, pealing, bubbling over with joy. Heads turned. The source was Fricka McCardle, and the gaze she trained on the man at her side was as exhilarated as her laughter. The man at her side was William Ellsworth.

Amelia turned away, and her eyes met Suzanne Longman's. What she saw there was a reflection of her own thoughts; for once she found herself wishing that communication between Suzanne and herself was a little less perfect.

Part Three

13

At fifteen, Miranda Upjohn stood a rangy five-foot-six, three inches taller than her mother, Amelia's sister Jacqueline, and an inch taller than Amelia herself. The height and build came from her father, along with a mane of heavy, straight, blue-black hair and almond-shaped black eyes.

"I couldn't believe it when Mom said you agreed to come and baby-sit me," Miranda said, folding herself gracefully into the VW. "I mean, you must have lots better stuff to do and all."

"Not really." Amelia embraced her niece, got as enthusiastic a response as the cramped space permitted, and feared for her rib cage. She had catapulted to the top of Miranda's chart years ago when she had responded to "Who's the greatest Mets position player ever?" with "Keith Hernandez" and had never lost her rating. "If you grow much taller I'll have to get a new car."

"I think I've got my full growth. Mom hasn't had to put a mark on the wall for three months." Miranda laughed. "I never thought you'd come."

No more had Jacqueline when she telephoned evening before last, frantic because the regular sitter had come down with appendicitis practically on the eve of a bankers' convention in London that Jacqueline had been looking forward to for months. She was reluctant to grant Miranda's request to stay with a friend. "Cindy's mother drinks too much—and worse, I think. Rather than have Miranda stay in that house, I'll give up the trip. I know it's short notice, and spending a weekend in scenic New Jersey won't be much of a treat, but you're my only hope." The appeal would have been hard to resist even if Northvale hadn't been a minefield full of mementoes of what Amelia was trying her damnedest to forget. Gabriel had laughed and called her a soft-hearted sucker, but he hadn't really minded being deserted for a few days, especially since she had promised to pack the freezer with chicken pesto, *blanquette de veau,* and other goodies from the Well-Tempered Cleaver.

"Cindy's going to be awfully disappointed," Miranda said. "Not to have me stay with her, I mean. I don't suppose you'd go for having her sleep over tomorrow night?" Hopeful.

"Sure. Why not?"

"Great." A thoughtful silence. "I don't suppose you'd go for skipping ballet class? Just this once?"

"No. I wouldn't." Amelia had been briefed that her niece's enthusiasm for ballet had waned since she had made her high-school baseball team.

The response to this was a sigh of resignation but no further argument. Amelia dropped Miranda at the ballet studio, where no watchers was a strict rule, then parked the car and did some shopping: Merrill Ashley's *Dancing for Balanchine* and Thomas Boswell's *Why Time Begins on Opening Day* at a bookstore; *The Thirty-Nine Steps* at a video store; dark Russian rye bread, sesame rolls, croissants, baklava, and chocolate cake with mocha frosting at a bakery. Returning to the studio, she found the street crowded with double-parked mothers. Miranda was practically the first one out the door and spotted the VW at once, so they were able to make a quick getaway.

Amelia congratulated Miranda on making the baseball team. "Your mother says you're the only girl who did."

"The only *position* player," Miranda corrected. "Wendy Siskin's on the team, too. She's a pitcher. Awesome sinker."

"You must be over the moon."

"Yeah." A deep sigh. "One small problem. Mom won't let me

114

give up ballet, even though I don't care about it anymore. Well, maybe a little, but I'd rather spend the time taking infield practice. Do you think you could talk to her?"

"I could. But I think the one who needs talking to is *you.* Presumably you beat out everybody else at second base because you have the agility and flexibility to turn the double play. Where do you suppose you developed those skills? Didn't you ever watch Gregg Jefferies klutz it up around the bag and wonder if a bit of ballet training might have helped him? I know I did. Lots of times."

Miranda giggled. "He wasn't exactly smooth, was he? You've got a point, Aunt Amelia. If I quit ballet I might lose some of the moves. I'll think about that."

Possibly she did, but she didn't broach the subject again during Amelia's extended weekend visit. An enjoyable visit, because keeping up with a bright adolescent didn't allow much time for brooding. Saturday morning was devoted to baseball practice (Amelia was invited to watch), and in the afternoon Cindy Patterson appeared, a rabbit-faced, quiet girl who showed no signs of the depravity Jacqueline attributed to her mother. Amelia drove the girls to Riverside Mall, where they looked at clothes, jewelry, CDs, videos, and turned up their noses at the lot. Later, they ate at a Chinese restaurant and went home to watch *The Thirty-Nine Steps,* new to both girls and given thumbs-up in spite of its age. Sunday morning Cindy went home and Wendy Siskin, a strawberry blonde who looked like a centerfold in embryo, arrived for some soft tossing in the backyard, staying on for lunch and a Mets spring-training game on television. Later, Miranda opened up in a heart-to-heart ("If I work really, really hard, do you think I have a chance of becoming a professional ballplayer?" "Only if you're ten times as good as any guys around." "Yeah, I know. Sometimes I wonder why I bother." "You know exactly why you bother." "Yeah, I guess I do."), and they watched *The Thirty-Nine Steps* again. Monday morning Amelia drove into Manhattan to have lunch with Val Stern, who remarked that Amelia looked tired but didn't belabor the point and insisted on ordering champagne to celebrate a big-bucks advance for the outpourings of the mediumistic Englishwoman; she also promised to post off more work without delay. Later, Amelia watched Miranda's infield practice and, much later, long after Miranda had finished her homework and gone to bed, the Upjohns came home, and the three of them sat up almost till dawn talking about London.

Tuesday morning Amelia set out for home, freshly aware that outside of Northvale was a whole world and feeling more connected to it than she had in quite some time. On impulse, she made a detour to the Lower East Side and Isaac Gellis, filling the ice chest with corned beef and pastrami and tongue and salami and frankfurters, cole slaw and sauerkraut and potato salad and pickles—the works. A treat for Gabriel, who, like all transplanted New Yorkers, complained about missing all those good delicatessens. Now they could feast for a week, and to hell with the cholesterol count.

Back home, there was a fine film of dust overlaying all the surfaces, as if the house had been uninhabited, and the gourmet treats provided for Gabriel were still in the freezer. But, reassuringly, there was a small heap of dirty dishes in the sink. Amelia unpacked the ice chest, arranging the contents on plates and bowls and covering them with plastic wrap, just about filling the refrigerator and having to admit to herself that very likely she had overdone it. She poured detergent over the dirty dishes, filled the sink with water, and went upstairs to unpack. All at once the short night and the long drive caught up with her, and she stretched out on the bed for a short nap. The next thing she knew, Gabriel was bending over her, stroking her hair, telling her how much he'd missed her, how glad he was to see her.

"Really?"

"Really."

"Put up or shut up."

He laughed. "You're on."

Later, she said, "I should go away more often."

"No." He took her hand and brought it to his lips. "I need you. I don't know what I'd do without you."

She stroked his hair in reply, thinking (not for the first time) how utterly unpredictable he was. For weeks and weeks—months even—not a word of affection would pass his lips, and then, out of the blue, a burst of verbal ardor. Not that she really needed to be

116

told he cared about her. Still, it was nice to hear him say it once in a while.

Gabriel gave her hand a squeeze and released it. "I must be getting old. The spirit is up for a return bout, but the flesh isn't. To be candid, I'm famished. I think I could eat the proverbial horse."

Amelia assured him he wouldn't have to, and they went downstairs in their kimonos to raid the refrigerator. His appreciation of the haul from Isaac Gellis was every bit as exuberant as she could have wished. "I want some of everything," he announced, and heaped up his plate. She exercised a bit more restraint.

When Gabriel slowed down enough to talk, he confessed that this was the first decent meal he'd had since she'd left. "I'm so spoiled I couldn't face scratching up meals for myself. I ate out most of the time. Jesus, I never want to see another hamburger or taco."

She laughed. "Maybe you'll turn vegetarian yet."

"Don't hold your breath. I'd have to be reborn as—Oh, speaking of reborn, you missed a hot news flash. It seems that Eliot Parking will be having a sex-change operation over the summer. The word's all over campus."

"Good God! I know the man thrives on publicity, but—"

"Not this time. He didn't advertise it, he was spotted in Boston coming out of the office of a doctor who specializes in pre-op counseling, hormones, whatever it takes, and he had to fess up. Everybody's wondering whether *his* tenure will carry over to *her.*"

Amelia laughed. "Who came up with that one? Silvia Bianchi?"

"It hasn't been officially credited. What else have you missed? Oh yes—Pam Blair. It seems she's going to have the last laugh on Northvale. She's signed a contract on the lecture circuit for molto bucks."

Amelia feigned surprise. "Good for her." Too enthusiastic—Gabriel raised an eyebrow. "Well, you have to admit she got a raw deal."

"That she did." He grinned. "You'll note that I'm not such a total company man as to deny it."

"Noted."

"I'll even go so far as to show you the 'Nuisance' piece on it. They had a field day, as you might expect." He put down his sandwich and pushed his chair away from the table with obvious regret.

"Sit and eat. I'll get it. Briefcase?"

"Briefcase."

Amelia got up and went to the table just inside the front door, where Gabriel always dropped his briefcase the minute he came in. She searched inside for the *Northvale News,* found it, and pulled it out. Gazing out at her was a photograph of Pam Blair at her fiercest, captioned NOT GOOD ENOUGH FOR PREPPIE PLAYPEN, GOOD ENOUGH FOR REAL WORLD. Amelia smiled and unfolded the paper.

And gasped. Gazing out at her from the other half of the front page was a photograph of Henrietta Hazelton, captioned PROMINENT CITIZEN MOURNED.

Everything blurred. Amelia stumbled to a chair and sat down. For a moment the room seemed to sway around her. She focused on the stoneware cylinder of the lamp beside the chair until it stopped moving. Everything stopped moving. She looked again at the newspaper that was still, amazingly, in her hand. The print was no longer blurred, it was sharp and distinct. She was able to read that Henrietta Hazelton was dead after a long illness, had died peacefully in her sleep. Clear. Concise. Comprehensible.

Amelia couldn't believe it. She forced herself to read the words again. And again. They came out the same way each time.

"What's taking so long?" Gabriel asked. "You can't possibly be lingering over the style. There isn't any."

"I—I haven't read it yet. I got sidetracked by the article on Henrietta Hazelton's death. It's—it's sort of a shock."

"It is, isn't it? The old bat was practically a Northvale institution. One expected her to go on forever. But apparently the real reason for the wheelchair wasn't arthritis, it was a bum ticker. That's the scuttlebutt, anyway."

A bad heart. A legitimate cause of death. Hastened, no doubt, by the stress of recent events.

Stop it, Amelia told herself. You are not not *not* responsible for this death.

"Amelia?"

"Just getting to the piece on Pam, darling." She hoped her voice sounded less edgy to him than it did to her. "They never waste an opportunity to stick it to the college, do they?"

Gabriel laughed.

Amelia let her breath out slowly. She had succeeded in fooling him. Wow. What an accomplishment. Quickly, she skimmed the article on Pam. No surprises. You could count on the "Nuisance" for total predictability. Now for sitting back down at the table for some repartee about who would be turning green with envy at Pam's success. Could she handle it? Sure she could handle it. She was becoming an old hand at deceit, wasn't she?

14

Amelia had done the breakfast dishes, swept, vacuumed, and had just donned rubber gloves and dipped a sponge in baking soda solution to scrub the bathroom tiles when the phone rang. The temptation to ignore it was strong, but she dropped the sponge, peeled off the gloves, and went to pick up the extension in the bedroom. "Hello?"

"Mrs. Cunningham?" A woman's voice, measured, confident, not young.

"Yes."

"Elizabeth Hearne at Duquesne and Franzen. We represent the late Henrietta Hazelton. She left an item in trust for you."

"For me? But—"

"Her instructions were quite precise. I've been trying to reach you for several days. Would it be possible for you to stop by the office today?"

"Of course. What time would be convenient?"

"Noon?"

"I'll be there." Amelia hung up, wondering. And was glad she didn't have very long to wonder. There was just time enough to finish cleaning the bathroom and make herself presentable.

The offices of Duquesne and Franzen were on South Maple,

on a block where lawyers' offices stood end-to-end on both sides of the street (Amelia sometimes speculated on the amount of litigation that must go on to support them all). The building was two stories high with a white clapboard exterior, as were most of its neighbors. The outer office had cream walls, a rugless waxed board floor, slat-back chairs, and a solid oak desk presided over by Elizabeth Hearne. Short and stocky, with a Buster Brown thatch of salt-and-pepper hair, dressed in a bronze tweed pant suit and Bass oxfords, she was as no-frills as the setting. The item in question was a slim nine-by-twelve manila envelope "delivered to us two weeks ago. She knew she didn't have very long, you see."

Amelia said she saw, presented the requested ID, signed a receipt, stowed the envelope in her shoulder bag, and was out of the place in no time at all. The minute the door closed behind her, she was tempted to take out the envelope and rip it open. Amazing how much willpower she had to muster to walk to the car and get in and drive back home. The bag was a magnetic field.

What had Henrietta Hazelton felt compelled to say to her at the end? She was overwhelmed with curiosity. Curiosity—and dread. She didn't know what she was afraid of. Hardly likely, after what had passed between them, that there would be deathbed recriminations. What else was there to fear?

Nothing. Everything. Take your pick.

The phone was ringing as Amelia entered the house. She let it ring. She went over to the sofa, took the envelope out of her bag, sat down without removing her coat, ripped the envelope open. Inside was a computer printout.

Dear Amelia:

The circumstances under which you will receive this require no explanations and very little in the way of preliminaries. I apologize for the ugly appearance of this missive. It has been some time since I have been able to hold a pen, and I must rely on this state-of-the-art machine. Usually I entrust correspondence to my secretary, but in this instance I felt it necessary to dispense with an intermediary.

If I read you correctly, my dear (and I think I do by now), you will have asked yourself whether our stressful conversations might have precipitated my end. You may rest assured that they did not. It has long been beyond the power of anyone or anything to affect the progress of my affliction. I have given out that it is arthritis, but it is not, it is something even more debilitating. For years I have watched myself disintegrate by millimeters. The most the doctors have been able to do is advise me that when I begin to have difficulty breathing it won't be long. Assuming that they are correct, I estimate that the time remaining to me is not more than a few days. It will be given out that I died of heart failure. True enough. Everyone's heart fails at the end.

In a sense I have been fortunate. I have been granted more time than most to resign myself to my own death. I have done so. What I cannot resign myself to is Katherine's, and that, of course, is the reason for this communication.

It occurs to me that for someone who professed to see no need for preliminaries I have been slow to get to the point.

When last we talked, you will remember, I was perfectly willing to accept the idea of William Ellsworth's being a murderer: to my mind he already was one. However, like you, I was bothered by the lack of a convincing motive. It might not have been much of a marriage, but they appeared to have reached a sort of accommodation. Plainly, Katherine had long since ceased to be an impediment to his hedonism. In fact, having a wife he could claim not to be able to leave might have been an asset rather than a liability. Why kill her? Of course no outsider can ever know the truth of any relationship, and I thought it perfectly within the realm of possibility (though loyalty prevented my suggesting it to you) that Katherine had in some way provoked William beyond measure. On the other hand, it was equally possible that Katherine's accepting stolidity was only a mask, that every little adventure of William's was torment for her, that she monitored his mail to keep tabs on him, that the prospect of being pilloried as the chronically betrayed wife drove her over the edge.

I have always prided myself on my fair-mindedness and my objectivity. These qualities cannot be shucked off in an instant. My heart—my soul, if you like—believed that William Ellsworth was a murderer; my mind harbored just that smidgen of doubt.

That doubt is gone now. Amazing, isn't it, what discovering the existence of a strong motive does for the perspective? The discovery was purely fortuitous. An antiques dealer in Boston whom I've known for many years telephoned me to find out what I could tell him about a Goddard-Townsend kneehole desk that had just showed up at Sotheby's, offered by an unknown owner in Northvale. I don't know how much you know about American antique furniture, but I can assure you that Goddard-Townsend are top of the line. They were a pair of eighteenth-century cabinet makers in Newport, Rhode Island, whose work was very distinctive, characterized by block front and shell construction, among other things. Now, American kneehole desks of the period are extremely rare, and the chances of there being two Goddard-Townsends that dealers don't know about in a small place like Northvale are slim, to say the least. I happen to know of one. Katherine's. It has never been on the market. Purchased originally by a merchant ancestor, passed down from generation to generation—you know the sort of thing. If Katherine had ever got round to making her will, she would have left the desk to one of her nieces. A given, and a strong argument against suicide, to my mind. Be that as it may, my dealer friend says the desk at Sotheby's is almost a replica of one in the Yale Gallery of Fine Arts; so is Katherine's. Any doubts I might have had were dispelled by the information that a collection of Canton porcelain, also from Northvale, arrived at

Sotheby's at the same time. You may be sure I asked for particulars. It is unquestionably Katherine's collection.

I should inform you that a Goddard-Townsend knee-hole desk that wasn't quite as fine as Katherine's went for half a million some years back. It would bring much more today. Add another hundred and fifty thousand for the Canton (a very conservative estimate), and we're talking about fairly serious money. While it wouldn't represent a fortune to many people these days, it would to William Ellsworth. Katherine once told me that his dream of paradise was straight out of a Gauguin canvas, a small house on a tropical island full of nubile girls. He's close to retirement. The haul from Sotheby's should make his dream a reality and enable him to gratify his appetites to his heart's content.

I am not an imaginative person, but I have no difficulty envisioning William seizing the opportunity presented to him by the anonymous letter. What is the alternative? A future in which Katherine putters in her garden while he molders away like Siegfried McCardle?

There you have it. Motive. The motive of all motives, if one is to give credence to the conventional wisdom. I no longer have the slightest doubt that William Ellsworth murdered Katherine. I pass that on to you for whatever it may be worth, knowing full well that what convinces me might not convince anyone else. In any event, belief is a long way from proof. And that is as it should be.

What you will make of this, my dear, I cannot begin to guess. You will, I am sure, think about finding proof. A hopeless task. Why, then, do I burden you with my speculations? Can it be that deep in my heart I cherish a hope that you will be able to perform the impossible? Perhaps.

I shall expunge this from the machine's memory. I request that you burn your copy when you have no further need of it.

God be with you.

HH

The printout fell out of Amelia's hand. Dropped to her lap. Slid to her knees. Wavered there. Stayed put. It wasn't going to let go of her.

A mandate from the grave? If so, binding. She would have to follow it.

How?

Assume that William Ellsworth had murdered his wife. Easy enough, now that profit entered the picture. Henrietta Hazelton was right. Establishing a motive made a world of difference. It compelled belief.

All right, then. William had murdered his wife. He shouldn't be allowed to get away with it. Somebody had to do something.

What?

Something. *Something.*

With a groan, Amelia leaned her head back against the couch and closed her eyes. Unwelcome thoughts were buzzing in her head like a horde of noxious mosquitoes. The reference to Siegfried McCardle in the printout concentrated them, an orchestrated buzzing she couldn't ignore. She remembered the moment at the spring-term inaugural party when she had spotted Fricka McCardle's naked adoration of William Ellsworth, and her eyes had locked with Suzanne's. She had succeeded in refusing to face the implications of that revelation, thanks mainly to the diversion of the trip to New Jersey.

No backing off was possible now. Assume William had murdered Katherine for gain. Along came Fricka, who had spent her youth as handmaiden to her brother and clearly longed for a future playing the same role for the man she idolized. How long a future was it likely to be? Presumably she owned her house and the contents of it (sure to fetch a tidy little sum in today's antiques market). Suppose a golden years union. Suppose Fricka died soon afterward. Would anybody wonder about it, think of cause and effect? Hardly. No doubt William would contrive a convincing accident for her. No doubt murder, like everything else, got easier with practice.

Farfetched? An edifice constructed of straw bricks? Sure. It was nothing but speculation. No reason to suppose that William had plans for upping his stake in that tropical island/bimbo future.

But would he be likely to refuse such incredibly easy pickings?

Amelia sat up straight and hugged her arms. She felt cold. She felt frightened. She felt as if she were on a runaway train that was gathering speed and there was no way to get off.

Had there ever been a way to get off? Hadn't it always been too late? From the moment she had opened her mouth and that toad of an idea had popped out, the train had started moving. Fast. Much, much too fast.

15

It seemed to Amelia that she was spending an inordinate amount of time watching the grass grow. Literally. She would drive past a patch of green stubble one day and, a few days later, there would be a veritable island of green. The annual cycle of death and renewal, taken for granted before, utterly absorbing now. A lesson there, perhaps. But what kind of lesson? Not one for her. With the death that was haunting her, there could be no renewal. It was final.

She couldn't settle down to work. Even the task of editing the manuscripts Val Stern had sent from New York—straightforward, rudimentary editing that as a rule she could perform almost in her sleep—was beyond her. Fortunately Val had said there was no rush. Restless, pacing the floor like a caged animal, Amelia seized any opportunity to get out of the house. But how many books could you take out of the library? And how many trips to the Grand Union or Pure Priorities or the Well-Tempered Cleaver could you make? The tried-and-true panacea for tired spirits, mounting a shopping expedition, was no use at all when you couldn't summon any interest in what was in the shops.

She decided to become a tourist for a while. Every morning, after Gabriel left for the college, she drew up an itinerary. And followed it. She visited the state house at Montpelier, the birth-places of Chester A. Arthur and Calvin Coolidge, the homestead of Ethan Allen. She spent an entire day exploring Addison County, learning that it was named for Joseph Addison of *Spectator* fame; that it was the birthplace of John Deere, builder of the Plow that Broke the Plains; that it was known during the nineteenth century as the Sheep Capital of the World. After a while, the historical villages with their steepled churches and town halls and clapboard houses clustered around a central common started to repeat on her, and she felt that she never wanted to see another covered bridge. And so she often found herself pulling over to the side of the road and stopping the car and gazing at the landscape. The occasional scrawny, tired-looking cow came within gazing distance, but no nearer. Once a swaybacked pony the color of rusty tin came up to the open window of the car, peered in, and apparently liked what he saw enough to remain for a while. When he left, he deposited a souvenir that forced Amelia to leave, too.

One morning, as she sat over her itinerary, she glanced out the window and saw snow falling. This was the thing about Vermont she never got used to. Here it was the start of April, the Major League baseball teams were breaking camp and heading north, and it was snowing. But Vermont weather was no respecter of the baseball calendar. She recalled a day some years back when she had listened to a game from Fenway Park, huddled under a down comforter (the furnace had been on the blink), while outside the snow was pounding down. The scene outside now was nothing like that, rather a lazy, feather bed–shaking descent of flakes, but snow was snow. One landmark looked much like another under a white blanket.

She decided that this would be a good opportunity to explore the Shelburne Museum, to which she had once paid a token visit, promising herself to return and somehow never quite getting around to it. Today would be the day. She would dress up a bit, make an occasion of it. Black cords, tall black leather boots, her favorite burgundy cashmere turtleneck sweater (actually, her only cashmere sweater—the black one she'd had since college was no longer fit for anything but KP and garbage detail), a reasonable amount of makeup. Toss on her black leather jacket, and she was ready to go.

A few minutes after she set out, it stopped snowing and, as she approached Shelburne, she could see no sign of snow anywhere. In fact, the sun was visible and climbing, and the day looked as if it had never been anything but fine. Amelia wondered whether she should pass up the museum in favor of an outdoor activity. A ferry ride, perhaps. The thought did nothing for her. She decided to continue on to Burlington, check out the doings on Church Street, find a nice place to have lunch, and cover the Shelburne in the afternoon.

It seemed like a good program at first. Church Street, Burlington's brick-paved, pedestrians-only thoroughfare, was generally busy, and the sudden appearance of a beautiful day assured a lot of happy faces on view along with the carts selling tatty ethnic clothing and message T-shirts and jackets, jewelry made with rocks and seeds and wood and leather and bone, foods that smelled and looked like guarantees of heartburn or worse.

A shop window caught her eye. It belonged to a gallery she was unfamiliar with, and the attention-grabber was a painting of what looked like pale sand with a seven-toed footprint the color of pimiento. Possibly an Australian aboriginal artist? The name on the card, full of bunched vowels, was inconclusive. Amelia's curiosity was sufficiently piqued to lure her into the shop. To her immediate regret. The walls displayed other works of the same painter, and they were all busier and more representational and less successful, cut-rate Gauguin with an overlay of Hollywood and travel ads. She wanted to leave, but her entrance had drawn someone from a back room, a stringy-haired, granny-glassed female waif who looked like a reincarnation of a sixties flower child from a distance and a fossilized version of the species up close. Amelia felt obliged to hear out the sales pitch—the painter was Samoan, a distant cousin of Greg Louganis, self-taught; this was his first show outside Samoa—and to make suitable responses. Worst of all, she had to waste time pretending to scrutinize the paintings.

"Amelia! Amelia Cunningham. What a delightful surprise."

Ice formed along Amelia's spine. She turned her head. William Ellsworth was standing in front of the door the waif had come through, a canvas under his arm.

"Hello there. Wonderful to see you," she said, with an attempt at brightness. And cringed inwardly: it reeked of insincerity.

He came toward her, tall and trim in cords and elbow-patched tweed jacket, hair like polished silver, a smile tempering his finely tuned features. As usual, every inch the gentleman scholar. Amazing that he hadn't suddenly sprouted horns or a tail or showed some other sign of the selfish, sensual, murderous bastard she now knew him to be. His smile was sunny, welcoming, totally free of embarrassment. She forced herself to smile back.

"You're just in time to vet my purchase. It's primitive, but I'm afraid I couldn't resist." He held the canvas, which was protected with a clear plastic seal, out for her to see. A pair of bronze girls in flower-printed sarongs washing laundry in a stream, oranges and hot pinks and golds and greens and blues almost neon bright but somehow harmonious, and certainly arresting.

His dream of paradise was straight out of a Gauguin canvas, a small house on a tropical island full of nubile girls. . . .

Amelia's stomach turned over. She knew she had to say something, but her tongue seemed to cleave to the roof of her mouth.

She forced it free. "Very . . . striking." Lame as well as late. "The painter has a very vivid sense of color."

William Ellsworth laughed good-humoredly. Either she had passed muster or he didn't give a damn what she thought of the picture. He remarked that the purchase had made his morning, a morning devoted to errands of exceptional tedium. Running into Amelia was another stroke of good fortune—he was facing the prospect of a solitary lunch.

That set her tongue going. Fast. She babbled that she was running late, she couldn't possibly stop for lunch, she had come to Burlington for a stoneware vase she had seen in January but unfortunately it was gone, she had already spent more time than she should have window-shopping, blah, blah, blah. It was graceless. It sounded like bullshit. Worst of all, launched against his flawless display of courtesy, it made her feel guilty.

Guilty. Self-contempt kept her company on the way home

(for of course there was no longer any question of the museum or any other outing). Why the hell should *she* feel guilty? *He* was the murderer.

Was he? Confronting him like that, polite, affable, imperturbable, she had trouble fitting the murderer's cap on him. Who wouldn't? Suzanne. Henrietta Hazelton. A very short list. Maybe they were wrong. Whatever, she hadn't done Gabriel any good, blushing and stammering and gurgling in front of the head of his department like a schoolgirl. No. Schoolgirls these days had more poise.

Like a preschooler. Like a barbarian.

Well, she would have done better if she hadn't been taken by surprise. No question. No question at all.

What were the tedious errands that had brought William Ellsworth to Burlington? Trying to peddle Katherine's jewelry, perhaps? Or her silver? Bad guess. He wouldn't try that so near home. Boston would be safer. Better yet, New York.

Amelia realized that she was taking William Ellsworth's guilt for granted. She also realized that she was driving too fast. She slowed down. If only she could slow down her mind, which was still traveling full tilt on that road to nowhere.

16

She was climbing Brangaene and it was a hard climb, much harder than she remembered. Had the hill grown since the last time she had climbed it? Absurd. Most likely it only seemed steeper because the perspective was different at night.

Then why was she panting?

Maybe it wasn't Brangaene she was climbing at all. Maybe she had lost her way and it was a different hill altogether. Possible. In the ghostly moonlight anything was possible.

The peak at last. Ahead, an expanse of velvety grass and the woods looming beyond. Familiar, even by moonlight. She was on top of Brangaene after all.

She had to reach the woods. Imperative. She didn't know why, knew only that something terrible would happen if she didn't.

Hurry. She had to hurry.

Downhill now. Fast, fast, fast. God, it was steep. Too steep to take at this speed. She almost seized up, just like the time in Stowe when she had let herself get talked into skiing down a slope too advanced for her. Then she had somehow forced herself to relax, go with it. She had made it then. She was making it now.

Level ground. Safe to accelerate. She was running like the

wind now. But it wasn't fast enough, she was sure of that. She could see her shadow running ahead of her. Suddenly there was a bigger shadow gaining on her shadow, swallowing it up. . . .

Amelia awakened and sat bolt upright, as if she had been pulled by an invisible string. Beside her, Gabriel groaned in his sleep.

She held her breath, fervently hoping he wouldn't wake up.

He groaned again, muttered something, but slept on.

She let out her breath slowly, and immediately began to shiver. She hugged her arms.

Okay. So she'd had a nightmare. So what? Nightmares didn't necessarily mean anything.

Didn't they?

Sure. They meant your mind wasn't at peace. Well, that wasn't exactly a hot news flash, was it?

The shivering fit subsided. Now her heart was giving her trouble, pounding like a gong, drowning out the ticking of Gabriel's alarm clock. This, too, subsided. She heard the ticking again, loud and clear. Amazing how such a tiny clock could make so much noise. Yet somehow it wasn't intrusive. Companionable, rather. No doubt because she'd become all too familiar with it of late.

Maybe, if she closed her eyes and tried to relax, sleep would come. Sometimes it did. Not often, but sometimes.

She eased herself slowly into a recumbent position until the down comforter was covering her up to the neck. The sheet underneath her was still warm. Which meant it was time to put away the comforter and get out the cotton patchwork quilt. Past time, probably—one more thing she hadn't been paying enough attention to. Tomorrow she would start her spring cleaning. Turn the house upside down.

She yawned. Her eyelids felt heavy. Good. Against all her expectations, sleep was descending on her again.

And then she was falling. Not the usual dream plummet. She was falling with excruciating slowness, through air thick and viscous, like mud or molasses. Nonsense. Air couldn't be like that or else how could she be breathing?

Sure enough, she began gasping for breath, choking—

This time her thrashing around woke Gabriel.

"What's up?" Yawn. "The house burning down or something?"

Amelia's breath was coming in deep, shuddering gasps. She shook her head, unable to speak.

He slid his arm around her. "Nightmare?"

She nodded.

"Must have been a whopper."

Her breathing was almost back to normal. "Big whopper." She eased into the hollow of his chest. "Hold me, Gabriel. Tight. As tight as you can."

"Risky. You might have trouble breathing again."

"So what?"

He laughed and wrapped both arms around her, squeezing hard but not too hard. She burrowed into her cocoon. Snug. Safe.

It crossed her mind that once upon a time she wouldn't have had to ask him to hold her. Childish quibble. What did it matter whose idea it was? He was holding her, wasn't he?

Then why the hell should she feel as if they were two strangers clutching one another for solace during an air raid?

You're out of your mind," said Suzanne.

"I've thought and thought. It's the only way," said Amelia.

"It's no way at all. It can't possibly work."

"I don't see why not."

Suzanne picked up her lighted cigarette from the green marble ashtray and stared at it. "You'll have noticed that I'm out of the closet now. Couldn't hide it from Hal forever. Turns out he's been a secret pipe smoker for years. Amazing all the things spouses manage to keep from each other, isn't it?" She took a deep puff and let the smoke out slowly, grudgingly.

The big, airy, light-filled kitchen was silent, except for the ticking of the numberless free-form marble clock on the wall. I'm becoming excessively conscious of clocks these days, Amelia thought, gazing out the french windows at the glass-enclosed patio, where a wealth of greenery spilled out of stoneware planters and vases and bowls (seconds from a now-defunct pottery for which Suzanne had created slip designs).

"It's a crack-brained idea. All the way."

"What if it is? What's the alternative? Don't tell me, I know. I should try to put the whole thing behind me and get on with my life. Well, I've tried, but I can't. I feel I'll never be able to unless I'm a hundred percent sure he killed her."

"I am."

"No, you're not. Any more than I am. Ninety percent, maybe."

"Ninety-nine."

"All right. That's not really the point anyway. The point is, it bugs the hell out of me that this man who probably committed murder goes blithely on with his life while the two of us are so burdened with guilt we can hardly hold our heads up."

"You do turn a phrase nicely, Amelia." Suzanne took another suicidal drag on the cigarette and crushed it out. "I wish I could say there's more poetry than truth in that summation, but it's fair enough. Your mistake is thinking there's anything we can do about it."

"But I just told you—"

"I don't need to hear it again. What good would it do to send him another anonymous letter? Do you seriously expect him to be so shaken by it that he'll rush to the police and confess? Or maybe you envision the guilt festering in him until he can't bear it any longer and has to proclaim his sin on the village green like what's-his-face in *The Scarlet Letter*."

"Arthur Dimmesdale." Amelia had to smile. "And you're always telling me you're not a reader."

"They force that one down your throat in school. It wouldn't work, Amelia. Most likely our sainted William will give that charming chuckle of his and toss the letter into the wastebasket."

"I don't think so. If he killed her—and we're ninety-nine percent sure he did—then he has to be the one who destroyed the envelope the letter came in. So he has to realize that somebody else knows it was addressed to him, not to Katherine—the person who sent it. However confident he may feel, there has to be a part of him that's been expecting the other shoe to drop all along. He wouldn't be human otherwise."

"Okay. I'll concede that much. So what? Why should he worry? He knows nobody can prove a thing."

"Essentially, the threat would be exactly what it was the first time round—disclosure. You know as well as I do that's something to reckon with in Northvale, not to mention the college. Even scandal about peccadillos has been too much for some people to live down, and this— I think he might have a legitimate concern about his image. Where this letter would differ from the first is that it would get down to specifics and say that if he wants to keep his secret, he should wait for instructions."

Suzanne lit another cigarette; puffed at it thoughtfully. "A touch of blackmail to lure him into the open? Ingenious, but he's bound to smell a rat. Even if he doesn't, I'm inclined to think he would prefer to tough it out rather than pay blackmail. After all, he must be near retirement, and I doubt that he has anything to fall back on except his pension and the house."

"You're wrong there." Amelia took the printout from Henrietta Hazelton out of her purse and shoved it at Suzanne. "You'd better have a look at this. Then we can do as she asks and burn it."

Suzanne started reading. After a moment, she looked up at Amelia, eyes wide with surprise, then looked down again. "I wouldn't be in such a hurry to get rid of this if I were you."

"Why not? Practically every word is engraved on my brain."

Suzanne finished reading, took a deep, slow drag on her cigarette, crushed it out deliberately, all without looking up. "A Goddard-Townsend desk is a big, big deal—I've met dealers who would kill for one. I'll bet she had a few things besides the porcelain that could be cashed in, too."

"I wouldn't be surprised. There's no question he stands to gain enough for a cozy retirement to the tropical paradise of his choice. Tahiti. Barbados. Maybe Samoa. I ran into him in Burlington a few days ago with a Samoan beachscape tucked under his arm."

"Complete with seminaked nymphettes? Cute. Well, it's certainly a motive. The motive of all motives, as the lady says here." Suzanne looked up, her face somber. "You've got balls, Amelia,

I'll give you that. Bearding Henrietta Hazelton that way. Not many would have."

"I knew she was Katherine's friend, and after I talked to you—Well, I was hoping against hope that you were wrong, that against all the odds Katherine had really taken her own life. Ghastly enough, God knows, but the alternative was so much—"

"And I suppose you told La Hazelton everything?"

"You mean about *you?* Of course not. What do you take me for? Hell, Suzanne, I haven't even told Gabriel!"

"I just wondered. Sorry. I should have known better. How did she react?"

"Well, the first time I went to see her she gave me short shrift. But she loathes William Ellsworth as much as you do and after she thought about it she asked me to come back and—" Amelia took a deep breath. "Not that any of it matters now. I'm figuring that if I make the demand relatively modest—say ten thousand dollars—he'll go for it."

"Make it five. He's cheap. Okay. Let's say he buys it. Let's say you arrange for him to make the drop. What then? If you have any ideas about getting the police to stake out the site—"

"No. I've thought about that, of course, but I'm sure they wouldn't take me seriously. They'd probably think I'm fantasizing out of guilt because I'm the one who sent the letters or something. As far as they're concerned it's suicide, open and shut. No. I thought if I photograph him making the drop and take the pictures and the money to the police—"

"Not really evidence. Most likely they'll say the only one guilty of a crime is you."

"I'm hoping they won't. I'm hoping I can convince them there's something to investigate, and if they investigate they'll find a way to nail him. Damn it, he shouldn't be allowed to get away with it!"

"No, he shouldn't." Suzanne picked up the printout and held it over the ashtray. "Now?"

"Now."

Suzanne lit a match and touched it to a corner of the paper. The flame traveled quickly, and in a moment she had to drop the paper. Another moment, and it was a heap of ashes.

"There's something else gnawing at me, too," Amelia said. "It started at the spring inaugural, when I saw the way Fricka McCardle looked at William Ellsworth. As if the sun rises and sets out of his eyes."

"That's nothing new. She's been mooning over him for years. It's such an old story nobody even talks about it anymore."

"It's become current again, hasn't it, now that his marital status has changed?" Amelia remembered the knitting class where everybody was dying to talk about Fricka's open secret, but refrained out of courtesy to her. "You know, seeing them together like that, I had an overpowering sense of déjà vu. I knew—I absolutely *knew*—that once upon a time Katherine had looked at him exactly the same way. Later, after I got that"— she gestured at the heap of ashes—"I started thinking about history possibly repeating itself. After all, Fricka must be fairly comfortably off and she worships him. What if he marries her and—Do you think that's reaching too far?"

"Damn it, no. He might decide he wants a few more palm trees or maybe even a whole island. If it worked once why shouldn't it work again? Poor Fricka. I never thought the day would come when I'd hear myself saying *that*." Suzanne sighed. "What exactly do you want from me, Amelia? Surely not editorial assistance."

"In a sense, that's what I do want. I didn't really read the anonymous letter carefully, just got the gist and then Tom Tracy took it away. I need details, so I can make mine match. What computer did you use? What kind of envelopes? And could I see a copy of the letter to check points of style?"

"I used one of the public-access computers at the college, legal-sized white envelopes you can pick up in any stationery store or even in the supermarket, and all my copies went up in smoke a long time ago." Suzanne gave a tired, mirthless smile. "But I guess I can reconstruct it from memory. You're not the only one who has things etched on the brain."

17

WELL YOU THINK YOU GOT AWAY WITH IT BUT YOU'RE WRONG. WE
BOTH KNOW THAT YOUR WIFE DIDN'T KILL HERSELF OVER AN ANON-
YMOUS LETTER THAT WAS SENT TO YOU NOT TO HER. WE BOTH
KNOW THAT YOU KILLED HER. PRETTY SOON EVERYBODY WILL
KNOW. YOU AND YOU ALONE CAN PREVENT THAT. INSTRUCTIONS
WILL FOLLOW. MEANWHILE REPENT.

Amelia had second thoughts about "you and you alone"—
maybe overkill?—but they came too late. After she had typed the
letter on one of the college's public-access computers, printed out
a label addressed to William Ellsworth, Esq., sealed up the envelope and dropped it into the mailbox outside the Northvale post
office. The words were as good as written in stone now.

How would William Ellsworth react to the letter? Would he
take it to the police and tell them the resident pest was active
again? If he did, surely she would be the first person the police
would question, or at least near the top of their list. Not that there
was any way they could prove anything against her. Half of
Northvale used the college computers, and she had worn gloves
handling the printout and the envelope. Still, she couldn't help
wondering whether she would be able to issue a denial without
giving herself away.

Probably it wouldn't come to that. Probably William Ellsworth wouldn't want to expose an accusation of murder to the police, put ideas in their heads.

But if he did? It would mean either (a) he was innocent or (b) he was supremely confident that nothing could be proved against him. She wouldn't be likely to find out which. Ever. Should the police enter the picture to investigate the new anonymous letter, she was out of it. Completely. For good. There would be nothing more she could do.

Nothing more she could do. Such a nice, final ring to that. It almost held the promise of release. Illusory, of course. No real possibility of release for her anytime soon. She was on the hook to stay.

The immediate problem: how to keep from going nuts. To keep from staring at the telephone as if it were alive. To keep from rushing to the window every time an engine sounded in the distance to see if the police were coming to question her.

Amelia tackled her spring cleaning. The usual first step, going through the clothes closets and deciding what to discard (and taking a firm stand against the pack-rat instincts she and Gabriel shared), required more cerebration than she was capable of just now. Yet skipping it would mean things that probably should have been got rid of ages ago would be kept around for another year. Compromise. Pull everything questionable, take the lot downstairs to the storage closet, and make the final determination later. A good plan. Before she started pulling, she rifled Gabriel's pockets (he had a habit of stuffing them with scraps of paper—notes for work and lectures, daily agendas, receipts, anything and everything) and tossed the contents into a brown paper bag, to be sifted later. She came across a folded piece of strawberry-colored paper and wondered where he'd picked it up, but her curiosity was resistible and it went into the bag with the rest.

The preliminary weeding took a considerable amount of time. Amazing how many clothes they owned that they never wore, and, because both their closets were divided into summer/winter halves without regard to frequency of use, garment-by-garment scrutiny was required. In Gabriel's closet, there were numerous sport jackets he was always saying he wanted to get rid of, some left over from an earlier lifestyle but most sent faithfully by his mother under the misapprehension that casual wear in semirural New England was the same as in the suburbs (could she have seen the assortment of jeans and cords, hacking jackets and Buffalo Bill jackets he habitually wore she might have had kittens). Amelia pulled three jackets from the winter side of Gabriel's closet (including a gray one with a metallic thread woven into it) and four from the summer side (including one of powder blue shantung that looked like what to wear to inaugurate a bowling alley) and tossed them on the bed. From her own closet, she pulled a shantung sheath, a linen suit, a mohair-and-wool Chanel jacket and matching skirt, a calfskin envelope bag, calfskin pumps—all navy, all substantial investments during a previous life. She would take the lot to the Northvale Thrift Shop. Never mind "You never know." She did know she could live happily ever after without wearing navy again.

She took the clothes and the brown paper bag downstairs to the storage closet and returned upstairs to start the cleaning. A very physical cleaning. She would scrub and scour and polish until she had just enough energy left to slap up a respectable dinner and get through it without lapsing into coma. Then maybe she would be too exhausted to dream. Maybe.

She set to work. Scrubbing. Scouring. Polishing. The police did not telephone. They did not come driving up to the door. Suzanne had declared herself "two hundred percent certain" that William Ellsworth wouldn't go to the police. "But give it a week—better yet, ten days—before you hit him with the follow-up. Let him sweat it out. In the meantime, business as usual for us." The last had sounded even more meaningless than it usually did: Amelia had all but forgotten what "as usual" meant.

The one certainty she held on to during her cleaning binge was that if the police didn't come near her, it meant that William Ellsworth hadn't reported the anonymous letter. Only when she had finished cleaning upstairs, most of the downstairs living space, and was finishing up the kitchen area, when the furious physical activity was winding down and her mind beginning to stir from its torpor, did she ask herself whether the certainty was really so certain after all.

Suppose William had reported the letter. Suppose the police, instead of getting in touch with her, were watching her to see what she would do next. Suppose right now there was a stakeout car lurking somewhere along the road to town, waiting to follow her anywhere she might choose to go.

No sooner did she have that flash than she had to check it out. Abandoning her cleaning with the downstairs looking like the site of a jumble sale (Gabriel would be in for a shock if he popped in unexpectedly), she tossed an old khaki raincoat over her ammonia-drenched sweatshirt and jeans and went out to the car. She drove slowly down the narrow winding road; speeded up some but not much on the road into Northvale.

No car appeared in her rearview mirror. No motorcycle either. In the center of town, traffic was heavy, as always in the late afternoon. She crawled along Principle Street, part of the parade, then turned right at St. Xavier's Church and headed out of town, away from home. Surely this would be the acid test. For a while she shared the road with commuters, until she reached the turnoff for the long, rugged road, full of potholes, leading up to Lookout Point. Once the Point had been much frequented for the view, but in recent years Little Mount had found greater favor with tourists, even boasting a tearoom-cum-gift shop. Amelia expected to have Lookout Point to herself. If another car came anywhere near hers, she would have plenty of cause for concern.

No other car approached. Not in the space of the ten minutes she forced herself to watch the dashboard clock mark off, sitting taut in the seat, hands gripping the steering wheel. The time passed with agonizing slowness. Only when it was up did she allow herself to unwind. She leaned back against the seat and closed her eyes, willing her neck to relax, then her shoulders, her upper arms, her elbows, her fingertips. . . .

When she opened her eyes, gold was spread across the sky, shot through with streaks of deep peach and orange. A glorious Vermont sunset was in progress and, alone on her hilltop, Amelia felt almost as if the panorama were a private screening. She watched the colors change. Flame. Red. Deep rose. Magenta. Purple. Deep blue. Finally, darkness. It was time to leave. More than time. She would be very late. She thought about the mess she had left behind her in the kitchen and wondered what she was going to tell Gabriel. That she'd had a sudden attack of claustrophobia in the middle of cleaning? Plausible. And she would suggest dinner out. Chinese. Her treat.

She didn't have to tell Gabriel anything. There was a message on the answering machine that he would be late. She had plenty of time to tidy up the kitchen and prepare a macaroni/cheese/ham casserole to pop into the oven the minute he walked in the door.

The next day Federal Express delivered four manuscripts from Val Stern "to be edited and returned to me *tout de suite*." An insider's view of a current rock group by a woman whose spleen suggested that she was a discarded groupie. The memoirs of a former Congressman who knew everybody in Washington, also splenetic and extremely spiteful. A blueprint for American businessmen on how to avoid being swallowed up by the "Yellow Peril." A biography of George Eliot so dull it was hard to imagine who would want to read it, unless the recent appearances of *Silas Marner* and *Adam Bede* on "Masterpiece Theatre" had stirred up a groundswell of insatiable curiosity about the creator's mildly scandalous life.

Hers not to ask why. Hers only to correct, tighten, and, where necessary, reorganize and restructure. Routine. Something Amelia could do with half her brain, provided she could subjugate the other half, which threatened to give way to panic. It took effort. It took exertion of self-control she didn't know she possessed. It exhausted her. And yet, however tired she was at night, sleep was rarely dreamless, rarely restful.

The agreed-upon ten days passed. On the last night, Amelia had the falling/suffocating nightmare again, and spent the small hours with George Eliot. In the morning, she telephoned Suzanne with a spur-of-the-moment invitation to go antique hunting. Exactly as planned, in case someone was tapping the phone or watching the house or whatever. They couldn't be too careful—they had agreed on that. She would pick up Suzanne and they would canvass a slew of antique shops in the North Country. Very much the sort of outing they'd often had in the past.

The past. Prehistoric times.

At first glance, Suzanne looked her old self, swaggering out of the house in the magnificent olive drab wool gabardine trench coat she had bought in Paris, her beautiful russet hair in a smooth, burnished coil at the nape of her neck. She folded herself up gracefully and slid into the VW. "I thought you would have changed your mind by now."

"No, you didn't."

Suzanne shrugged. Up close, strain showed. The flesh under her eyes looked bruised, and the lines at the corners of her mouth had deepened. "Let's make sure to cover that little place near Ferrisburgh. The last time I was there they had a terrific trencher. I passed it up because it cost a bundle. Maybe I shouldn't have. What the hell, you only live once. Right?"

"Right." Amelia started the car. She drove through the center of town, where traffic was light at this hour. "The police haven't come near me. I'm sure he didn't report the letter."

"I never believed for a moment he would. But I've been wrong before." Suzanne reached into her bag for a cigarette, lit it, pulled out the dashboard ashtray and dropped the match into it. "Looks virgin. Remind me to clean it out."

"Don't worry about it."

"I won't." Suzanne inhaled; blew smoke out slowly. "Have you given any thought to a site for the drop?"

"Yes. The statue of Mercury on the patio outside the skating rink. The space under his skates is big enough for a book-length manuscript, let alone a packet of money. Hardly anyone goes near the rink even in the daytime now that the hockey season's over, and nighttime trysts aren't likely to be a factor because the students will be on spring break next week. Two A.M. seems like a good time."

"I was thinking along the lines of a location out of town, but your idea's better and—" Suzanne stopped.

"And what?"

"Safer. It could be dangerous, you know."

"I don't see why it should be. The sentinel elms will give me

144

plenty of cover, and you said it's possible to take photographs at a distance without flash bulbs."

"That's the least of it. Hal got some fantastic pictures of a Hopi snake dance using a telephoto lens and high-speed recording film. I can lend you the equipment and show you how to use it, but"—a hesitation—"at crunch time you'll be on your own."

"I know." Amelia did know, and yet, at the sound of "crunch time," she shuddered involuntarily.

"You don't have to go through with it."

"Yes I do. It has to end, once and for all. I won't have any peace until it does. My mind, my body, every part of me is in turmoil. I'm all bits and pieces, spinning around without direction. Even when I'm asleep I can't get away from it. I have nightmares. I'm either being pursued by a faceless, shapeless something I can never confront, or else I'm falling into a void as thick and stifling as molasses. I want the turmoil to stop. I want the nightmares to stop. I can't help feeling that it won't be over for me till I've done everything I can to appease Katherine's spirit. Whatever it takes."

"Maybe not even then," Suzanne said softly. "Some things never go away."

"Thanks a lot. You're a great comfort."

"Did you expect comfort?"

That didn't require an answer, and Amelia gave none. Neither of them spoke again until they reached the first port of call, a shop specializing in antique tools (Suzanne's interest) and antique kitchen utensils (Amelia's interest, in a mild sort of way), where they made polite noises for the benefit of the proprietor and didn't linger. The second shop was better, with some fine pieces of country furniture on view, including a hickory comb-back Windsor chair that Amelia would have gone wild over and very likely splurged on had she really had antiques on her mind. The third shop had the trencher that Suzanne remembered from a previous visit. It was a huge chunk of rough-hewn pine, painted dark green on the outside, astronomically priced, and it just about filled the back seat of the VW. They visited three more shops, and in the last Amelia picked up a redware pitcher that under other circumstances would have sent her into orbit; today the spurt of joy she felt in buying it gave way almost at once to guilt.

They stopped at a roadside market for tofu-and-sprouts sandwiches on pita bread and banana yogurt shakes, pulling off the road a bit further along to eat. Not that the idea of a picnic lunch had much appeal, but a restaurant was hardly the place to draft a blackmail letter.

"This time coyness would be a mistake," Suzanne said. "Direct and determined."

"I agree. How about: 'Thursday morning at two A.M. bring package containing five thousand dollars to Mercury and—' "

"Five thousand dollars in small bills. Very important."

"Right. 'Five thousand dollars in small bills to Mercury and place under skates. Leave at once. If you fail to follow instructions exactly police and press will be told—' "

"Make it 'police, press, and everybody in Northvale.' Reputation is really the only thing he has to worry about. God knows nobody can prove a thing."

"Okay. 'Police, press, and everybody in Northvale will be told that you killed your wife.' " Amelia sighed. "It sounds pretty feeble. He'll probably find it eminently ignorable."

"I doubt that. I've been giving this scheme of yours a lot of thought. While I haven't changed my mind that it's pretty dippy, I have to admit that you just might jump-start his motor. Gossip can nail you to the wall in this town even if the college does its usual sweeping under the rug. William has always struck me as somebody who gets off on bamboozling people. I think he'll be worried. Amelia—" Suzanne swallowed the last of her drink and crushed the container in white-knuckled hands. "It really could be dangerous, you know. There's no telling what he might do if he feels threatened."

"I'll have to risk it. Anything's better than this overload of angst. Feeling that I should do something and doing nothing. No wonder I'm having nightmares. I want the whole business to be over, once and for all. I want the wounds to heal. I want to be able to start growing some scar tissue."

"You want too much." Suzanne began wringing the crushed container. "There are no guarantees. You think you've put something behind you, and boom, it leaps up and bites you. Before I hooked up with Hal I led sort of a rackety life. Had a couple of abortions. I didn't think anything much about them at the time—like having my tonsils out. A few years later, when I was carrying Sara, the nightmares started." Suzanne stared out the window at the mountains, her hands wringing, wringing. "Always the same nightmare. I'm minding a houseful of kids and I put them to bed in a big room like a dormitory and tuck them all in. Then I go into the kitchen to make apple pie. While I'm slicing the apples, I notice the house is very quiet. Too quiet. I go to check on the kids and I find them all lying there with plastic bags over their heads. I run from bed to bed like a madwoman, pulling off those plastic bags, but it's too late. They're all dead, and their flesh is as chilly as marble. Then I wake up."

"Suzanne." Amelia put a hand over Suzanne's moving hands, wanting the agonizing action to stop.

It did. Suzanne's hands quieted under Amelia's touch, then pulled out from under. The crushed container fell to the floor.

"Yeah." Suzanne turned to face Amelia, her eyes hard and bright. "I think the trencher will make a great cornucopia at Christmas, don't you? Wrong shape, but the basket I've been using isn't stable. When I fill it up, it's apt to tip over. Woke me up last year, going bump in the night."

"Terrific idea." Amelia started the car, though the sandwiches had barely been tasted. Headed back to Northvale, to put an end to this parody of an ordinary day.

18

On Friday, Amelia typed the blackmail letter on one of the public-access computers at the college, typed a label for the envelope. Ready to go.

On Saturday, she posted the letter in the after-hours mailbox outside the Northvale post office.

On Sunday, she went on a book-hunting expedition with Gabriel. They covered what seemed like most of western Vermont, visiting bookstores, flea markets, yard sales. Gabriel found, among other treasures, a tattered, moldering copy of Hall Caine's *Recollections of Dante Gabriel Rossetti,* which he had coveted for years. That sent his spirits sky high, and Amelia feigned similar rapture at finding a good hardbound copy of Mary Kingsley's *Travels in West Africa.* They had a leisurely dinner in a restaurant offering a spectacular view of Lake Champlain and a less than spectacular cuisine. Amelia couldn't have asked for more in the way of distraction. If only she could have been distracted.

On Monday, she woke up with a great weight pressing down on her forehead. She tried to lift her head, and the room began to spin. Could it be that her brain was copping out of facing the day? She closed her eyes and counted to a hundred, added an extra fifty for good measure, opened her eyes and tried again to lift her head. Same result.

She closed her eyes; dozed lightly until Gabriel stirred beside her and muttered his usual greet-the-day obscenities. She forced her eyes open. Even with her head stationary, the room was moving.

"Do you think you can handle breakfast for yourself? I'm having the most awful attack of vertigo."

"Flu."

"Couldn't be. My throat's not sore. And my nose isn't stuffed."

"This strain's different. Vertigo. Nausea. It's been sweeping through the college like a tornado, flattening people right and left. You'll feel like death today and most of tomorrow."

"Oh my God."

Gabriel planted a light kiss on her forehead and eased himself up off the bed. "Cheer up. By Wednesday you'll be fine."

That's what you think, she retorted. But only in her head, where nothing would ever be fine again.

She heard Gabriel clattering around downstairs. Didn't hear it anymore. Drifted into stupor. Drifted out. Time passed. Rapidly yet interminably. The chinks of daylight penetrating the slats of the shutters didn't vary, so she had no idea how the day was advancing. If she turned her head she could see Gabriel's bedside clock. She didn't turn her head. She didn't move a muscle. Didn't know she could move if she wanted to. Didn't want to find out. It seemed as if she had been in this near-vegetable state forever, had never known any other. . . .

Then the chinks of light left her. Then Gabriel was bending over her, asking her if she wanted anything (stupid question—what could she possibly want?), telling her he would sleep in his study, touching her forehead with a hand that felt like lead. . . .

She dozed. Floated into empty gray space. No bottom. No moorings. No danger. Nothing. As far as she could see, nothing. Only that vast, vast space, without color, without substance. No. There was something. Materializing in the distance. A body. Floating as she was floating. Coming closer, growing larger. A woman's body. Something weird about it. The head. Misshapen.

Distorted. Of course. There was a capsule over it. No, not a capsule. A plastic bag. Visible through it, a face, contorted in agony. She knew that face. Katherine Ellsworth's face. She screamed, but no sound came out. Katherine's body floated past. Only the empty gray space remained. The void. She was floating through it. Gently, so why worry? But the movement was downward, becoming less gentle by the moment. She was falling. Fast. Faster. The void was thickening around her, acquiring density, choking her. . . .

Amelia sat up in bed, gasping for breath. The void was inside her now, rising thick in her throat. She flung the covers off and staggered to the bathroom, her head reeling. She got the toilet seat up just in time, vomited up the obstruction in her throat in a searing, foul-smelling stream. It stopped. She flushed it away. But she was still choking. She waited for another upsurge. There was none. She had cast up everything inside her. Only the husk was left, dry and burning.

She moved to the sink and splashed water on her face. Icy, but offering no relief. She leaned forward and pressed her forehead against the mirror above the sink. That didn't help either, but she didn't move because she couldn't summon the strength to move. She closed her eyes, lest they adjust to the dark and see what there was to see in the mirror. Not to be borne. No way.

She was conscious of her sour breath. Could she manage to brush her teeth? No. The prospect of that fresh, minty taste in her mouth made her want to retch all over again. She settled for gargling with baking soda in water. It tasted horrible. She felt horrible. A match.

She staggered back to bed, and immediately a great cloud darker than darkness wrapped itself around her and carried her away. When it let her go, sunlight was penetrating the slats of the shutters. She was able to turn her head to look at the clock. Almost two. She had lost Monday and a large chunk of Tuesday.

Not much cause for regret. Monday would have been a day of torment—endless wondering how William Ellsworth would react to the letter. If ever there was a good time to come down with flu, this had to be it. Memory stirred, cast up an image of a blonde girl with a Hitler's-youth haircut and granny glasses who used to state

150

categorically that people never got sick unless they wanted to. Martha something-or-other. A girl Amelia had known in college, dismissed as a silly twit with silly theories, relegated to the limbo of submemory until now. Which went to show—what? That you couldn't be sure of anything, maybe.

Slowly, gingerly, Amelia lifted her head from the pillow. The room didn't move. She sat up again, exercising caution. Swung her legs to the floor. Everything stayed put.

She got out of bed and walked to the bathroom on legs that threatened to give out on her any second. She wouldn't let them. She felt clammy and grubby, and it was essential to deal with that immediately, spaghetti legs or no spaghetti legs. Somehow she managed to brush her teeth without gagging on the toothpaste. She forced herself into the shower under a spray sharp as sleet; soaped herself with a washcloth that sandpapered her skin. Shampooing her hair seemed to take forever. Emerging from the shower, she was exhausted and sore all over, but she felt clean. She wrapped herself in the bath sheet and patted herself dry. This, too, seemed to take forever.

How long she spent drying her hair, getting dressed, stripping and remaking the bed, carrying the soiled bedclothes downstairs and stuffing them into the washing machine she didn't know. It seemed like hours. Astonishingly, when she looked at the clock it was only twenty past three. Unfair. Just because she was going in slow motion, did the clock have to keep pace?

She went to the refrigerator, more because she knew she should try to get something inside her than because she really wanted to. Something bland. Like a soft-boiled egg. Or chicken soup.

Yuk.

Maybe yogurt? She opened the refrigerator door, and the first thing she spotted was a small can of grapefruit juice. Her favorite, but Gabriel disliked it, as she disliked pineapple juice, his favorite, so they routinely had orange juice in the morning, with the small cans stocked for private indulgences. She opened the can of grapefruit juice and took a cautious sip. Her stomach protested mildly, then accepted.

Sipping slowly, she sat down to watch television; found a tennis match between two men she had never seen before. The winner, it was announced, would play Stefan Edberg, who was Val Stern's idol ("best ass in the game as well as the best volley"). Amelia's interest ended long before the match did. She shut off the television, put the empty can on the floor, and curled up in the armchair.

The next thing she knew, the room was flooded with light and Gabriel was standing inside the door. He did a double take. " 'Holy Saint Francis, what a change is here.' You were practically comatose this morning."

She smiled. "A miracle, clearly."

"Clearly." He came over and stooped to kiss her forehead. "Sorry I'm so late. I decided to tidy up some odds and ends at the office and made do with pizza. I would have telephoned, but I thought you'd still be out of it. Have you tried eating anything?"

"Just some juice. I think I might be able to handle something a bit more substantial now. Maybe some yogurt and honey?"

"Sit still. I'll get it for you."

And he did. Yogurt nested in a creamy porcelain bowl, honey drizzled lavishly over the top. Her stomach rumbled at the sight. A positive sign—she was actually hungry. She thought, spooning up the yogurt and honey, that nothing had ever tasted so good. And having Gabriel fuss over her was nice, made her feel like a pampered kitten. She basked in it, knowing full well that it wouldn't last, that eventually reality would hit her hard. Never mind. Sufficient unto the hour. As long as it wasn't now.

They watched a video of *Charade,* which was funny and charming and still absorbing even when you knew how it would turn out. Gabriel suggested that he should spend another night in his study, and Amelia, feeling exhaustion settling upon her, agreed. Sleep came promptly, and it was deep and long and dreamless.

The telephone woke her at twenty past nine. Suzanne, wanting to know what time she was coming to pick up the camera. "Zero hour's approaching, you know."

"I know. I wouldn't have left it so late, but I've had the flu and lost Monday and most of yesterday."

"Lucky you." Suzanne's laugh was brittle.

"Eleven?"

"Fine."

Amelia got out of bed, feeling surprisingly full of ginger, without a lassitude hangover. Still, she would try to take it easy all day, so her energy wouldn't give out before tonight. Or, more accurately, early tomorrow morning.

Zero hour.

Suzanne had the camera all ready, fitted out with the telephoto lens and loaded with the high-speed recording film. The procedure, she said, was so simple a six-year-old could handle it. Amelia said the average six-year-old these days probably had greater mechanical aptitude than she had, and would Suzanne take her through the basics, just to be sure? Suzanne did. Amelia said thanks, she thought she was on top of it, and waited to be told yet again that it wasn't too late to back out, that she didn't have to go through with it. But the expected words didn't come, and the omission was disquieting. Which was absurd. There was no question of backing out—Suzanne was simply conceding the fact. Still, Amelia left feeling as if she'd been cast adrift to sink or swim. But why put that on Suzanne? Once the plan was in operation, she was really and truly on her own. Nothing Suzanne or anybody else could do for her. She had known that from the start.

There was knowing and knowing, obviously. Hardly a thought to induce comfort or cheer through what was surely going to be a long, long day.

Amelia spent some time shopping, some more cleaning the house, which required only perfunctory attention after the turnout she had just given it. She considered working in the yard, but decided against it. Gabriel's territory. Not that he was rigid about it—many a time she'd pitched in with raking or mowing or weeding—but the prospect of contact with growing things made her think of Katherine Ellsworth. She considered cooking a goulash to freeze for emergencies, and decided against it; in her present state she was likely to reach for the cayenne instead of the paprika or do something equally stupid.

She remembered the carton of clothes she had put away for donation to the thrift shop. She had asked Gabriel to go through it, but he had said whatever she decided to get rid of he would never miss, which was true enough. Same went for her stack of navy treasures of yesteryear. She would give the lot one last look and toss it.

On top of the carton of clothes was the bag of papers culled from Gabriel's pockets. He hadn't wanted any part of that, either. "Chuck the lot," he'd said. But of course she knew better than that—God forbid she should be responsible for losing notes for an article or an important address or telephone number. She squatted and dumped the papers out on the floor.

A folded piece of strawberry-colored paper caught her eye. She recalled seeing it before, wondering where it came from. She picked it up and unfolded it.

> *Beloved—*
> *Had to let you know how I feel. Wonderful. Terrific. A million million plus at the bone. It's never been so good for me before. Never never never never NEVER. I'd like to say the earth moved, but I don't really know that. The Volvo moved—that I'm sure of.*
> *Soon. Please.*
>
> *C*

The paper fell from Amelia's hand. Pain struck her stomach, acute and deep, like a swift kick from an elephant.

Maybe she was jumping to the wrong conclusion. Maybe the paper was something Gabriel had picked up from the floor somewhere and stuffed into his pocket and forgotten all about. He was staunchly antilitter. How many times had she seen him pick up paper from a Manhattan sidewalk and hang on to it until he found a trash can?

She picked up the note again. The handwriting seemed to leap off the paper at her, big, bold, black, straight-up-and-down letters, easy to read. The kick was just as potent. She hadn't got it wrong. The note had been written to Gabriel. By a student, plainly. Who else would cram three sophomoric literary references into so few lines? They had made it in the Volvo. Of course. Where else would they have made it? Wasn't her own first time with Gabriel in a car? Back then it had been the cramped little

Fiat. These days he had a lot more space to maneuver—and a backseat. Concession to age, very likely.

Bitchiness wasn't going to help.

What could? He had betrayed her. *Betrayed* her. *Gabriel.*

Oh God. The room started to spin, and Amelia leaned forward, dropping her head over her knees. She could have sworn she felt the floor shift underneath her, as if the house had been shaken to the foundations. Ridiculous. Symbolism didn't become actuality just like that.

Did it?

She sat up straight, forced herself to focus on the window. The clouds outside were locked in place. No more vertigo. She got up, still holding the note. She took it over to her work counter and shoved it under the manuscript she was working on. Leaving the other papers scattered on the floor, she went to the closet, grabbed her camel-hair wraparound coat, raced out of the house to the car. She started the engine, took the hill at high speed. Where was she headed? Somewhere. Nowhere. Anywhere.

The unthinkable had come to pass. Gabriel: betrayal. Betrayal: Gabriel. Either way it didn't compute. Other people betrayed. Not Gabriel. He was better than that, damn it! She'd taken it on faith all along that he was better than that.

Without faith, what was left?

She was overreacting. Common sense told her that much.

Shit. How could she not overreact? What else could she do?

Try to be fair.

Fair. The word made her heart lurch in her breast, ready to leap up if she let it.

Fair meant asking herself what kind of atmosphere Gabriel had been coming home to lately. A wife in a permanent funk, exuding a miasma of guilt and despair. Could she blame him for turning elsewhere for a bit of fresh air, comfort, distraction, whatever?

Yes, she could blame him. She could damn sure blame him. But she could understand him, too. Naturally she could understand him. Wasn't such understanding part of any adult relationship? Of course it was.

All at once she felt six years old. When had she even contemplated the need for such understanding in connection with Gabriel? Never. Not once. "Understanding" was an abstraction. Something for other people.

Maybe she was blowing the whole thing out of proportion. Since when was a single lapse a threat to a solid relationship? Common sense said otherwise.

Screw common sense. How did she know it was only a single lapse? The note had begged for more. How did she know there hadn't been more? How did she know "C" was the only one? Gabriel had been coming home late a lot recently. Maybe the Volvo was twilighting as a mobile motel. Maybe—

No. Letting her imagination run wild was the worst possible thing to do. Get a rein on it.

Amelia speeded up the car. She had no idea where she was, knew only that the road ahead of her wound uphill, pretty steeply. Appropriate.

So okay. Gabriel had fooled around with one of his students. He wasn't the first, he wouldn't be the last. It would have been nice to go on believing that he was proof against the standard campus temptation, but obviously he wasn't. The conventional wisdom had it that when men stray, the reason is to be found at home. Well, the conventional wisdom couldn't be faulted in this instance. She had been a marital disaster of late—no denying that. Easy to construct the infidelity scenario. An after-class discussion prolonged over coffee, the girl's enthusiasm kindling a response in a man who knew he was going home to a zombie, and so on and so forth. All too easy.

But something was wrong with that scenario. Something she couldn't quite put her finger on.

She flashed back to the day she cleaned out Gabriel's pockets. Saw herself removing the strawberry-colored paper from the pocket of a pair of pants. Linen pants, hanging in the left half of his closet, where his summer clothes were.

Summer clothes. Winter had set in before she opened her big mouth, before the anonymous letters, before Katherine's death, before home turned into Misery Hall for Gabriel.

He hadn't worn those pants since last summer.

"No!" Amelia shouted.

All at once she was fully cognizant of where she was: at the top of a steep hill about to start the descent.

She closed her eyes. What would happen would happen. Let it. What difference did it make anymore? She felt the engine throbbing, surrounding her with a pulse as the car sped down, down, down—

"No!"

She opened her eyes, took a firm grip on the wheel, pulled over to the side of the road, shut off the engine. She was shuddering, gasping for breath.

Stupid, stupid, stupid. What if another car had come along? The driver would have honked, surely.

And then?

Unthinkable that she might have put someone else in jeopardy, because for a demented moment she had flirted with the idea of inviting the big bang.

Don't think about it, then. What was some hypothetical someone to her at this juncture?

Amelia started the engine and, slowly, cautiously, started for home.

19

In the dark bedroom, Amelia sat in the armchair near the window gazing out at the night, not all that much brighter than the room because of the thick mist veiling the crescent moon and the stars. Any minute the heavens might open up. Then what? She would never be able to photograph William Ellsworth dropping off the packet of money in a downpour. All she would have to show for the master plan would be a soggy pile of money. Worthless as evidence. If the rains came, she might as well skip going to the drop site.

Even as the surge of relief swept over her, the mist moved away from the moon. Fate. Destiny. Kismet.

The Moving Finger writes; and having writ,
Moves on.

No joy there, unless you could read the writing. Did your unconscious squirrel away everything you ever read just to cast it up when your mind lost direction? Lucky for her she wasn't a fan of *The Prophet.* Or Carlos Castaneda.

She looked at the clock. Twenty after twelve. The hands had barely moved since she had last looked. She was ready to go. She had been ready for hours, ever since she had persuaded a suddenly amorous Gabriel that she needed one more night by herself and sent him, grumbling, to his study. What an evening! She had sleepwalked through it. Robot Amelia, playing the role of the little housewife with mind, feelings, everything on hold. And it had been a turnon for him.

God help her.

God help the both of them.

No. Not now. She wasn't supposed to be thinking about that now. She had to be totally focused on the job ahead of her. Trapping a murderer was far more important than her domestic problems.

Domestic problems. What a quaint, old-fashioned ring that had.

Not now.

She looked at the clock again. Twenty-three minutes after twelve. She had planned on setting out at a quarter to one. Time enough to position herself.

Getting up from the armchair, she walked to the mirror above the chest of drawers and examined herself in the dim light. Clad in black from the beret that covered her hair to the boots that came up over her cords almost to the knee, she looked like an ad for catburglar attire. Against all the black, the pallor of her face was startling, and for a moment she considered darkening it with eye shadow or crushed eyeliner. Ridiculous. She wasn't planning to be on display, she would be behind a tree, waiting with the camera.

Merely thinking about it made the whole business seem curiously unreal, as if she were following a script for the kind of film she never went to see.

What was William Ellsworth thinking along about now? What was he feeling?

Her mind backed off coming to grips with that, just as it had been backing off ever since she had committed herself to the plan. William Ellsworth was no longer a person with thoughts and feelings to her; he had become the Murderer, an abstraction, something as devoid of humanity as a video-game target. She knew this was childish, but she couldn't help herself. Dealing with William Ellsworth the man and William Ellsworth the murderer simultaneously was simply beyond her.

Was the plan going to work?

"Oh God, please let it work. Please let me get this monkey off my back so I can stand up straight again. Please please *please.*"

She had said it aloud. In the night-silent house, it sounded like a shout. She held her breath, half expecting Gabriel to come running, wanting to know what the commotion was.

He didn't, of course. He could sleep through an earthquake.

Gabriel. The vast area of numbness in her breast where her heart should be came alive with a knife-thrust of pain. He had accepted Robot Amelia with the plastic smile as the real thing, had actually liked her. Was that to be her future? The noble little woman who sports the everlasting smile when her insides are crumbling to dust? Shades of women's magazines of yesteryear. Not to mention vintage weepy movies. Luise Rainer with the telephone. Margaret Sullavan. Maria Schell.

God forbid. Better a knock-down-drag-out with Gabriel. Better—

Not now. *Not now.* She had to focus now. She had to have all her wits about her.

What if she didn't go to the rendezvous? It really was idiotic, thinking she could trap a murderer. Most likely he would ignore the letter. Most likely—

Why the sudden attack of jitters? There shouldn't be anything to worry about. If she stuck to her game plan, she was safe enough. She would leave the car in the parking lot among countless others and walk to the skating rink and station herself behind a tree and wait, take the pictures and wait some more, pick up the money and go home. It all seemed foolproof enough.

But Suzanne obviously thought there was something to worry about. Maybe thinking there wasn't meant she was kidding herself.

So she was kidding herself. How else could she have geared up for this little enterprise?

One thing was for sure, if she didn't get a grip on herself right now, she would unnerve herself. Big-time.

She decided to go and stake out her position now, do the rest of her waiting on the spot. Once she was there, no chance of turning back, no matter how much of a panic she stewed herself into.

Please let it work. Please let William Ellsworth show up and make the drop. Then she could take the photocopies of the letters, the pictures, and the money to the police. From there on out, it would be their baby.

Please let it work. Please let it work. Please let it work. She made a litany of the words, murmured them over and over as she drew on her gloves, then picked up the black canvas tote bag and checked the camera. Suzanne had said it was ready to go, all she had to do was press the button. If it wasn't ready to go, would she be able to tell the difference? No. She wouldn't. She put the camera back in the tote very carefully.

Amelia tiptoed down the stairs. Left the house silently. Got into the car. The sound of the engine catching was almost deafening, noise to rouse the dead. She knew her overstretched nerves were deluding her, yet she half expected Gabriel to come rushing out of the house to ask her where she was going, and then the whole story would come pouring out, and then he would put his arms around her and say she mustn't go, the whole idea was mad, and then—

Delusion, all right.

She started down the hill slowly. Even without the mask of cloud, the crescent moon gave little light, and the trees alongside the road increased the gloom. Not a night to choose for a ramble.

All at once her headlights picked up an obstruction ahead. She put on the brakes. About twenty yards ahead, stretched across the road, lay what looked like a heap of old clothes.

Or a body.

Amelia's heart raced. She told herself she was imagining things, it couldn't possibly be a body. More likely a bundle tossed from a passing car.

What passing car? Nobody used this road—it was pretty much a private access road. But maybe that was why somebody had chosen it as a dump site. With the cost of garbage collection rising all the time, people would go to any lengths to dispose of rubbish. How many times had she heard workers at the thrift shop complain about finding the after-hours donation box stuffed with items that were growing mold?

But maybe it wasn't rubbish. Maybe some drunk had wandered up from the main road and was sleeping it off. Whatever the thing was, the narrowness of the road and the trees on either side meant she couldn't get round it. *Merde.* She would have to get out of the car and move it.

The click of the door opening sounded loud, preternaturally loud, and Amelia was sorely tempted to shut the door, back up, turn the car around, and return home.

Kismet again? The damned moving finger?

She got out of the car, leaving the door open, and walked up to the thing in the road, following her shadow. No movement. No sign of animation. Just a heap of old clothes—she had been right the first time.

She sensed movement behind her even before she saw the shadow looming up and swallowing her own. Just like in the nightmare, she thought. Her head exploded into shards of brilliant light, and the world went dark.

She came up through waves of nausea. Conscious of movement. Must be on a ship, she thought. No. In a moving car, and she was feeling carsick as she hadn't felt carsick since she was a little girl. In a minute she was going to have to ask the driver to stop the car so she could get out and—

No. Car sickness wasn't the problem. The cocoon was the problem. Or whatever it was that wrapped her so tightly, imprisoning her, smothering her. A blanket, from the feel of it. Rough, thick wool. Yes. She could smell wool. Definitely. And she could smell something else, too. A rich, fruity, autumn-leaf aroma. A familiar aroma. Pipe tobacco.

Full awareness flooded over her. William Ellsworth's tobacco. William Ellsworth's blanket. William Ellsworth's car.

Christ. What a fool she'd been.

She attempted to lift her hands from her sides and push the blanket away, but it was wrapped taut. She couldn't move her hands. She couldn't move her feet, either. Surprisingly, she wasn't gagged. She could scream if she wanted to. Scream her head off.

What if she did? Even if the blanket didn't muffle the sound, who would hear her except William Ellsworth? A scream might startle him into losing control of the car, a prospect that boded no good to her. Doubtful that would happen. The man probably had nerves of steel.

How could she have been so stupid? Why hadn't she foreseen the possibility that he would target her as the author of the blackmail letters? That instead of trotting obediently along to the drop site he would try to ambush her? Try—and succeed.

Because she had underestimated the opposition. Badly. Fatally, perhaps.

Not fatally. Not if she could help it.

Famous last thoughts? No. *No.*

Now that she thought about it, how could he have failed to target her? Wasn't she the first person he was bound to think of when the second anonymous letter arrived? So okay, her absence from the scene when the original letters were sent, plus her public exhibition of remorse over Katherine's death, had probably persuaded him, along with everyone else, that she hadn't been the one who sent them, or at least made him willing to give her the benefit of the doubt. And he might have continued to do so, had it not been for that chance encounter in Burlington. How she had blushed, stammered, been unable to look him in the eye—the memory was gut-wrenching now. Doubtless, when the second letter arrived soon after, he interpreted her behavior that day as the guilt of the novice blackmailer. But maybe even without that he would have zoomed in on her. Who knew?

Suzanne. Suzanne knew. Or at least suspected. Hadn't she warned Amelia to be careful, the plan was dangerous? If only she had expressed her misgivings more forcefully, pointed out the potential for danger in detail, instead of letting someone who was supposed to be a friend walk into—

Amelia forced her mind off that track. Suzanne wasn't to blame. Only herself, for being too dumb to be scared.

Well, she was scared now. Good and scared. With plenty of reason. There wasn't the slightest doubt in her mind that William Ellsworth intended to kill her. Having killed once, why would he balk at killing again to prevent his nice, comfortable existence from being blown to smithereens? Particularly when the victim this time was someone he thought was a blackmailer, the lowest species of life in anybody's book.

She had brought catastrophe upon herself and no mistake. What choice had she left him but to kill her?

How? Whatever he had arranged for her had to be something that necessitated a fairly lengthy journey to carry out. An accident of some sort, most likely. And her body would be left in some remote place where it wouldn't be found for a long time, if ever. So much for the theory that murderers found a method and stuck to it. Hard to imagine that he would travel so far to stage a suicide. Most likely doing what came handiest was the rule, in murder as in everything else in this world.

Strange to be contemplating her own death in terms of logic. Or logistics. She would have expected pounding heart, chattering teeth, drenching sweat, whatever. Instead, she felt almost calm. As if what was happening wasn't real.

Maybe it wasn't. Maybe—

No. She couldn't shut her mind off. William Ellsworth had ambushed her. Therefore he meant to kill her. Unless she did something. Unless she shook off this mental and physical torpor and got herself going.

Her hands got the message. They forced themselves from her sides, rotated outward, began to claw at the blanket. Uselessly. The wool was too thick, too densely woven. Probably top-of-the-line L. L. Bean camping gear. Proof against rain, snow, sleet, and fingernails. An impermeable cocoon.

Oh God. Maybe he was planning to toss her into Lake Champlain. Wrapped up like this, she'd go straight to the bottom. She began to shudder, anticipating the cold water against her flesh. Fought for control. Things were bad enough without letting her imagination run riot. It was unlikely that he would drop her into the drink. Bodies had an inconvenient habit of surfacing, no matter how heavily they were weighted down. No. An arranged accident seemed a far better bet.

To know you were about to die, to know you were helpless to do anything about it—the ultimate bottom line. But did she know? Somehow her brain seemed to have disconnected from the whole affair, as if it had nothing to do with her. Reasoning. Weighing the murderer's options. Why wasn't her brain sending signals to her body? Every atom of her being should be agonizing, protesting, revving up for a struggle. She shouldn't be lying here passive as a block of wood, she should be thrashing around, banging her heels, screaming, doing *something*—

No. If she made any kind of commotion, he would probably stop the car and knock her out again. She had to choose her moment. If she was right about drowning not being the fate William Ellsworth had planned for her, there had to be a moment when he set her free. However he meant to kill her, he wasn't likely to do it while she was swathed in a blanket. Until she was physically able to make a move, playing possum was the wisest course.

All at once, she felt an overpowering urge to scream. Make a noise. Prove she was alive.

Why couldn't she get mind and body and nerves in synch?

A more immediate problem was breathing. No fresh air was penetrating the blanket. Very likely that was the reason for the torpor and for the ache starting behind her eyes. Maybe if she held her breath as long as possible—

The car slowed down. Stopped. A door opened. Closed. Another door opened, and a current of cold air penetrated the blanket. Hands gripped her ankles, and she was dragged out of the car and dropped roughly on the ground; it was all she could do to refrain from crying out in pain at the impact. The car door closed. She was scooped up off the ground and slung over a shoulder. Movement now. Pretty fast movement. She concentrated on making her body limp. Playing possum. Biding her moment. She heard twigs crackle underfoot, and deduced that they were in the woods somewhere. Going in deeper and deeper, without a doubt. Would she be able to find her way out if she managed to get away from him?

Don't think about that. Think about one thing at a time. The Hansel and Gretel problem was down the road.

She was dropped again, on her back, and again it required an effort of will to refrain from crying out.

"Your self-control is admirable, Amelia. Useless, however. I know full well that I didn't hit you hard enough to put you out this long."

William Ellsworth's voice made Amelia shudder. Because it sounded so normal. Urbane. Slightly detached. Distinctly superior. The accents of the professor you couldn't fool so don't even bother to try. She felt utterly transparent. A woman of glass.

"Pity you didn't rest content with making yourself a nuisance." The voice took on a shade of this-hurts-me-more-than-it-hurts-you. "But no, you had to upgrade nuisance into menace. It was foolish of you to suppose that I would tolerate that. Very foolish. You underestimated me badly, I'm afraid. On the other hand, I seem to have underestimated you. I never believed that you wrote the anonymous letters because I didn't credit you with sufficient guile. Your charade of grief over being the unwitting cause of Katherine's death was masterly. It fooled everybody, including me. I dislike being fooled. A trivial point, I must admit. This conversation is a trifle one-sided, isn't it? I'm going to set you free now. You will undoubtedly be tempted to scream. By all means do so, if you like."

Amelia found herself being rolled over as if she were a sack of potatoes, and then the cold air hit her. Her first impulse was to move her limbs, see if they still worked well enough to allow her to curl up against the chill. She didn't give in to it. Passivity was the name of the game. Choose the moment. She forced herself to lie facedown, not moving a muscle.

"If you're thinking about surprising me and trying to make a run for it, I should think again if I were you. I have a rifle and I'm prepared to shoot you. It will be assumed that you were walking in the woods as therapy for an ailing spirit and were the accidental victim of a hunter jacking deer, whose failure to come forward to admit culpability will surprise no one."

Again Amelia had the sense of being transparent. Pedagogical one-upmanship. No wonder the man was dynamite in the classroom.

Belatedly, the full import of his words registered. He had charted the perfect murder. He could shoot her with impunity. Of course nobody would question that her death was an unfortunate accident, caused by someone illegally hunting deer at night.

Except Suzanne. Suzanne would guess the truth.

But what could she do?

"Sit up, Amelia. I have no desire to shoot you, believe me."

She didn't. Not for a moment. She knew she had guessed

right. The reason he wanted her upright was that shooting her in a recumbent position would, most likely, put forensic holes in the master plan. She weighed her options, and decided to obey him. He might well have a Plan B.

Very slowly, Amelia rolled over on her back. Blinking the pastiness out of her eyes, she saw that she was in a small clearing in the woods. Her lateral vision picked up William Ellsworth as a shape about ten feet away. She didn't look directly at him. Not yet. She wasn't ready for that yet. She eased herself up to a sitting position and folded her legs in front of her.

"That's better. It is always preferable to confront one's interlocutor, don't you think? You look distinctly the worse for wear, I'm afraid. A tad grubby. But then, that's appropriate, isn't it? Yours is a grubby little soul. When the blackmail letter arrived, I was outraged. Then I tried to deduce who sent it, and you were the obvious candidate, for a number of reasons. I considered going to the police, but that seemed ill-advised. I even considered paying, but I knew that it wouldn't be the end, only the beginning. I knew that you wouldn't let go until you bled me of the tranquillity I have envisaged for my declining years, and that, my dear, I simply could not allow. You should have known better."

"Apparently." She forced herself to look at him. He seemed totally relaxed, leaning against a tree, a magazine illustration of an English sporting gentleman in dark tweeds, deerstalker hat, leather gloves, a rifle with a strap tucked almost casually under his arm. Would he have the slightest compunction about gunning her down like a rabbit? No, she decided, he wouldn't.

"You have left me no alternative," he said, reading her thoughts again. "I have the highest regard for Gabriel, and I regret having to cause him pain. However, I doubt that he will miss you more than I miss Katherine."

"What a pity you can't bring her back to life as easily as you helped her out of it."

He shook his head sorrowfully, as if she were a slow-witted student who had given the wrong answer. "I didn't kill Katherine. Naturally, I hardly expect you to believe that. Nor do I care whether you do or not. In any event, it scarcely matters at this point. You have no conception of the forces you set in motion with your little foray into black humor, my dear. Pity you didn't have the wisdom to let ill enough alone, but then wisdom never did enter into the scheme of things, did it? That what began with you should end with you has a certain symmetry, as well as seemliness. Nonetheless, I confess that I should be extremely sorry to see that happen."

"I'll bet."

"Spare me the sarcasm. It's tiresome. Listen to me carefully, Amelia. I am not a bloodthirsty man, and no one has ever accused me of being unreasonable. If you can make out a case for my letting you live, I am more than willing to consider it."

Hope fluttered in her breast, even as her mind told her he didn't mean it, he couldn't possibly mean it. To him she was a cheap blackmailer, who would say anything, promise anything, sign an oath in blood even. How could he believe anything she might say?

"Are you serious?"

"Perfectly. The prospect of killing you is repugnant to me. I would welcome an alternative. Why don't we discuss this in a civilized manner? We might even have a drink on it." He reached inside his jacket pocket and took out a pint bottle of Dewar's.

The flutter was gone. The robust flavor of the whiskey would mask whatever he had laced it with. Barbiturates, most likely. They had worked with Katherine. Why abandon a winner?

"Thank you. I'll pass." She managed to keep her voice level. Just.

"Please. You'll feel much calmer." He moved away from the tree and approached her, holding out the bottle.

"Will I? I'm inclined to doubt that I would feel anything ever again."

"Surely you don't think—I see that you do. Well, I suppose I can't blame you. However, you're wrong. There's nothing in the bottle but whiskey. I hoped it might make you more relaxed."

"So I won't be quaking with terror when you pull the trigger? How humane of you."

"It is, actually. A moving target is always a bit problematic. A Winchester carbine doesn't make a particularly large hole, but it does cause considerable pain. Have you ever witnessed the death of a deer? I strongly recommend drinking the whiskey, Amelia."

"Forget it. If you want to kill me, you're going to have to gun me down and watch me die."

"Your choice." He restored the bottle to the pocket inside his jacket and took two steps backward. In an instant the rifle was in his hands, ready for action. "Stand up, please."

"No." She closed her eyes, not wanting to know what part of her he was aiming at. Her chest, probably. Or perhaps her head. What difference did it make? In moments she would be dead, and here she was playing guessing games. Because it didn't seem real. Because she couldn't imagine being dead. Well, self-deception couldn't do any harm at this point, could it?

A click. Safety catch? Did rifles have safety catches?

Amelia sucked in her breath.

A snap. A thunderous bang. Reverberating in her ears. Reverberating, reverberating, reverberating.

Impossible. Her ears were still working. How could her ears still be working? She was dead. Oh God, she didn't want to be dead, she wanted to live. Never mind that only this afternoon she was playing Russian roulette in a moving—

She wasn't dead. How come? He couldn't have missed her at this range.

Slowly, unwillingly, she opened her eyes. Saw that William Ellsworth was no longer leaning against the tree, he had slid down to a sitting position. The rifle lay on the ground beside him. His eyes were closed and he wasn't moving. There was a dark stain on the front of his jacket. Blood? Or whiskey? What did it matter? He was dead.

But she was the one who should be dead. *He* had shot *her.* Hadn't he?

She heard a crackling sound behind her. Footsteps. Someone was coming. She turned her head. The mystery was going to be solved. But it was no longer a mystery—she knew who it would be. And it was. Suzanne Longman came out of the trees, wearing olive drab fatigues that were probably army surplus but on her looked like sixties-boutique playclothes, carrying a rifle on a strap in her gloved hands. She walked up to William Ellsworth and looked down at him.

Amelia found her voice with difficulty. "He's dead, isn't he?"

"Of course." Pause. "It shouldn't be necessary to say that in another few seconds it would have been you, but I'll say it anyway. Just in case you're about to express any regrets."

"I'm not. They would be futile." Amelia knew thanks were in order—Suzanne had saved her life, after all—but she couldn't get them out. She took a deep breath. "You knew he wouldn't fall for the blackmail scheme. You knew he would guess I was behind it and come after me."

"I told you it was a dippy idea." Suzanne backed away from the body and leaned against a tree, the rifle tucked under her arm. Exactly as William Ellsworth had stood a millennium ago.

"Yes. You did."

"I also warned you that it could be dangerous." Suzanne sighed. "Okay. I held out on you. I never told you how dangerous. Since I intended all along to provide backup, it hardly matters, does it?"

"I guess not." But it did matter, and they both knew it. "You were a jump ahead of him all the time. Just out of curiosity, did you stake out his house?"

"More or less. Last night I put a tracking device on his car so I could follow him without being spotted—there's no other way to do it on country roads. He did exactly what I expected him to do."

"And the outcome? Did you expect that, too?"

Suzanne tensed slightly. "Let's say I was prepared for it. Why? Do you think you have any kick coming?"

"You saved my life. How could I possibly complain?"

They let that one hang. For of course Amelia did have cause for complaint. Being manipulated was always cause for complaint. Oh, the phony blackmail scheme had been entirely her own idea. With hindsight, an exceedingly stupid idea. But Suzanne hadn't discouraged it, she had latched on to it and incorporated it into a scheme of her own. Had she wanted it to end the way it ended?

Don't think about that, Amelia told herself. Not now. Not ever. It was over. Be grateful for that.

She looked at William Ellsworth, stiff and still against the tree. She saw and registered every detail of his appearance, down to the glazed-over eyes, though how this was possible in the faint moonlight she had no idea. Did one develop cat's vision in crunch time? Once again she felt she was on a ride that was totally out of control. Not a runaway train, as she had thought before. A toboggan. Downhill all the way.

But surely she had hit bottom? Surely there was no further down to go? Her brain gave the right answer. Her instincts refused to accept it.

"Amelia. *Amelia!* Snap out of it! We don't have time for this. There's too much to do."

"You're right, of course." God, it was hard to wrench her eyes from William Ellsworth, hard to accept that he wouldn't get up and walk away. "We should get moving. Or at least one of us should. I mean, someone has to stay with—with the body till the police get here. That's the procedure, isn't it?"

"You've got to be kidding." Suzanne moved away from the tree and came to squat beside Amelia, setting the rifle across her knees. "How can we go to the police? What can we tell them? That we turned you into a stalking horse, hoping he would make a move on you so we could make a move on him? How's that going to sound? I know you're all for telling the truth, the whole truth, and nothing but the truth, but there isn't a hope in hell they'd believe it." Suzanne paused. "Not that they'd be any more likely to believe anything else we might decide to tell them."

The toboggan hit bottom, hard enough to send shock waves coursing through Amelia's veins. She shuddered deeply; reasserted control. "What makes you think they wouldn't believe anything we say?"

"Because William Ellsworth's proclivities are an open secret. Because if we take responsibility for his death everyone's going to assume sex is behind it." Suzanne took a breath so deep it sounded like a death rattle. "Because, though Sara's convinced nobody knows about her thing with him, I'm not. I don't want her hurt again. I don't want her to hear people say her mother blew a man away because he mistreated her."

And how far from the truth would that be? Amelia wanted to ask. And didn't.

"There's no way we can go to the police, Amelia. Even if we came up with a story that would satisfy them, think about the political fallout. Hal and Gabriel are going to feel the heat, tenure or no tenure."

Amelia knew Suzanne was right, at least as far as Gabriel was concerned. After all the attention her recent actions had directed at him, a scandal like this might very well finish him in Northvale. For a moment her heart leaped at the prospect: he would suffer as he deserved to suffer for betraying her. She was instantly appalled at herself.

"What do you suggest we do? Turn our backs and walk away?"

"Yes. After we neaten up a little. Come on." Suzanne stood up, slung the strap of the rifle over her shoulder, and walked over to William Ellsworth's body.

Amelia got to her feet in stages. To her knees first. To a crouch. All the way up. Her legs felt so weak and shaky it was hard to believe they could support her. But they did, somehow. They even walked by themselves. Followed Suzanne for a few steps. Stopped. They didn't want to go any further.

"Can you manage the blanket?"

No, I can't, Amelia thought. But her eyes found the crumpled mound of wool on the ground and her legs carried her over to it. How could she possibly bring herself to pick it up? Just looking at it made her shudder.

"Hey! You're not going to pass out on me, are you?"

"No." Amelia forced herself to stoop and pick up the blanket. And staggered under the weight.

"It'll be easier to carry folded." Suzanne came over to take hold of two ends. Amelia grabbed the other two, and they backed away from each other, gave the blanket a vigorous shaking, approached each other, folded. In seconds, the blanket was a tidy package in Amelia's arms. Once a cocoon. Once a prison. Now just a heavy blanket.

Suzanne walked back to William Ellsworth, stooped to pick up his rifle. "That should do it. When they find him, they'll think he was walking in the woods and some hunter jacking deer shot him by mistake."

Amelia gasped. "That's exactly how he planned to dispose of me! But you know that, you must have heard him."

"No. I was too far away to hear much. Great minds think

172

alike, I guess. Let's go." Suzanne turned away and stalked out of the clearing into the trees. Amelia had to hurry to catch up but then had no trouble keeping pace: her legs wanted out of there in the worst way.

William Ellsworth's Audi was parked close to the road, almost obscured by an overhang of branches. A bicycle was on a rack attached to the trunk. The keys were in the ignition. Suzanne opened the door and yanked them out, walked to the trunk and opened it. A jumble inside—sleeping bag, poncho, frying pan, rubber boots, books galore. Suzanne shoved the rifle under the poncho, took the blanket from Amelia's arms and shoved it inside, closed the trunk. She returned the key to the ignition and shut the door, then stooped to remove something from under the left fender and put it in her pocket.

"That's it, I think. I can't see anything to contradict the obvious assumption when they find him."

What if they didn't find him? Amelia thought suddenly. And then: It might have been me. She moaned aloud.

"Amelia?"

"Sorry. I'm okay. Delayed shock, I expect." Amelia swallowed hard. "I—I haven't thanked you properly, have I?"

"Don't be a ninny. Come on, let's get out of here. The sooner we do, the sooner we can start trying to kid ourselves we've never been here."

Amen, Amelia pronounced silently.

Suzanne had parked her car far back in the trees, and it was slow going to the road. Once they cleared the trees, the speedometer started to climb, until Amelia couldn't watch it any longer. She stared out the window at trees, fields, rocks, the occasional cow, the occasional barn whipping by. That her thoughts, her feelings were roiling was no surprise. Shock, self-disgust, anger, fear, guilt—all these she would have to live with for a long time to come. But something else was in the mix, a profound disquietude. As if, in spite of having hit bottom so resoundingly, she anticipated a further descent. Very likely not being able to admit her part in tonight's horror accounted for it. Wasn't confession the prelude to atonement, to healing, to getting on with one's life?

No. It was something else. It had to do with William Ellsworth's denial that he had killed Katherine. Why should he have bothered to deny it at such a moment? Unless it was true. Unless—

The something started to take shape in her mind. A ludicrous shape. Damned if she'd let it. No more bringing monsters up to the light. Assume that William Ellsworth had wanted to cause her as much torment as possible. End of speculation. End of story.

The car slowed down, and Amelia saw that she was home. Or at least at the foot of the hill. Halfway up was her VW Rabbit, parked beside the road under a tree. Had William meant to leave it there? No. He meant to come back and drive it to the woods. That's why he had the bicycle.

Amelia began to shudder.

"Take a hot shower," Suzanne said. "As hot as you can stand. Amelia—" A pause, fraught with tension. "Remember that recurring nightmare I told you about? What I didn't tell you was why it started again after so many years." She took another of her rattling deep breaths. "When William dumped Sara, she swallowed a bottle of Seconal. It was only by a miracle she survived. Thea had gone to basketball practice without her lucky headband and came home for it and found Sara and got her to the hospital in time."

"Oh my God. Suzanne—"

"Don't say it. Don't say anything. It's over now. No other woman is going to put her head in the oven or OD because of that bastard ever again. Let's leave it at that."

"Suzanne—"

"I said leave it." Suzanne leaned in front of Amelia and flung open the passenger door. "You can oblige me by never never *never* mentioning it again. *Any of it.* Agreed?"

"Agreed." Amelia unbuckled her seat belt, got out, closed the door. As she started up the hill, Suzanne gunned the engine and roared off into the night.

Amelia approached the Rabbit cautiously, all too aware that William Ellworth had driven it last. What was spooking her? Certainly not fear of a bomb or a booby trap. Bad vibes? His aura?

She stopped. What if he had taken her keys and they were found in his pocket?

No. There they were in the ignition. And there was the tote

with the camera. Amelia heaved a sigh of relief, got into the car and drove it up the hill and around the house, parked it beside the Volvo.

Time to get a new car, she promised herself as she let herself into the house and crept up the stairs like the cat burglar whose garb she had appropriated. She went into the bathroom and switched on the light. In the mirror, huge black eyes stared out of a dead white face. Cat burglar? She looked more like the twin sister of Conrad Veidt in *The Cabinet of Dr. Caligari.*

Hot shower. She peeled off her clothes and stepped into the tub and closed the shower curtain and turned on the hot water— almost hotter than she could stand. She soaped herself, shampooed her hair twice, and stood under the burning spray for a long time. Turned off the water and got out of the tub and toweled herself vigorously. The mirror was fogged over, and all she could see was an expanse of flesh. Not quite boiled lobster. More like poached salmon.

By the time she dried her hair and put on her gray silk nightshirt, the mirror had cleared sufficiently to give her a good view of herself. Despite her heightened color, she looked as if she were wearing a shroud. She shut off the light and went out of the bathroom. At the bedroom door, she hesitated: the big empty bed looked like a lunar platform in the pallid light.

She turned away and went into the study. Gabriel was sound asleep, lying on his side in the middle of the sofa bed, his body a graceful curve under the blanket. She was tempted to lie down beside him and wrap herself around him from behind, as she often did.

She couldn't do it. All she could do was stand there and look at him. Even in sleep, he was gorgeous, profile taut and ivory smooth above the faint darkness of beard, hair slightly sleepmussed but none the worse for that. Gorgeous and elegant. Like a Renaissance prince.

And just as remote.

She tiptoed out of the study and into the bedroom. Climbed on to the lunar platform and closed her eyes, for all the world as if sleep were a real possibility.

20

The phone rang as Amelia was closing a suitcase. It was Millicent Neumeyer. "I hear you're leaving us."

"Yes. For a while. A change of scene is in order, I think."

"I rang to wish you good fortune and Godspeed. If there's ever anything I can do for you, let me know." Click.

Short and sweet. No Stand-Your-Ground-and-Fight pep talk, thank God. Which was a little surprising, come to think of it.

Even more surprising was how Millicent knew. Amelia hadn't told anyone she was leaving.

The last-minute packing was finished and she was heading downstairs with the suitcase in one hand and her overnight case in the other when the phone rang again. This time it was Silvia Bianchi. Amelia nerved herself to field a barrage of questions. But Silvia didn't ask any questions. She, too, had called to say goodbye. "I shall miss you, *cara.*"

Curiouser and curiouser. ESP? Or did the breezes waft secrets through the air? More likely Gabriel, in spite of his promise to say nothing until she was gone, had confided in somebody.

The third call came when everything that was going with her was stacked beside the door. This time it was Betty Frayn, wife of Gabriel's good buddy Alex and cook/homemaker nonpareil. Her good-bye was polite and stilted. Amelia could sense something building up behind it and hoped she was wrong.

No such luck. "Gosh, Amelia, I don't know what to say to you. I've never known. You always seemed so cool, so in control, and I've never been sure whether you knew or—" Betty stopped. "This is hard to say."

Then don't say it, Amelia begged silently. And said aloud, "Take your time."

"Right. Well—" A long silence. A regrouping silence. Then, in an entirely different tone, "Hey, you know all those local recipes I've been collecting? Well, I've decided to write a Vermont cookbook. I know you have connections in publishing and I was wondering—"

Amelia was only too happy to rush in with assurances that of course she would be glad to do anything she could, it sounded like a great idea. Betty said good-bye, and Amelia hung up feeling relieved. For she could guess what Betty had really wanted to say and hadn't been able to bring herself to say: "All those times Alex was supposed to be with Gabriel, I knew what he was really up to. Did you know what Gabriel was up to when he used Alex as an alibi? I've never been sure."

Conjecture of the most cynical order. Accurate?

Did it matter?

Gabriel, confronted with the letter, had admitted guilt readily. He had yielded to temptation. Once. He said the episode hadn't been repeated. Surely Amelia could forgive a momentary aberration? She said she didn't know. She needed time to think about it, therefore a temporary separation seemed like a good idea. She would go to New York for a while, shore up her professional contacts.

"You can't possibly be serious?"

"I can. I am."

"For God's sake, Amelia, don't you think we ought to talk first?"

"What is there to talk about?"

"Nothing, I guess." It was one of Gabriel's more endearing traits that he could cut off bullshit in midspout. "Telling you it

177

didn't mean a damn thing wouldn't make any difference, I suppose."

She said no, none. They agreed that she would remain in Northvale until the end of the school year, when her departure would be least conspicuous. And so, for the last few weeks, they had lived as housemates. Gabriel, to do him justice, had not tried to change her mind, unless grumbling references to "living in a jungle with a crack house on every corner and a mugger in every hallway" could be construed as attempts at counterpersuasion.

The only sticky moments had come last night. They had sat down to an ultracivilized dinner (chicken pesto from Terry Tracy, with steamed broccoli and cherry tomatoes; blueberries and sour cream for dessert), and afterwards Gabriel, pleading work, had shut himself up in his study. When she went upstairs to bed, he emerged to intercept her. For a moment she thought he wanted to make love one last time, but no, all he wanted was to ask her if she was sure she wanted to do this. Quite sure, she said, and he went back into his study, and that was that. Just as well, she knew. And yet she couldn't help feeling a pang of disappointment.

This morning Gabriel was gone before she got up to make breakfast. She found a letter on the table.

Dear Amelia,

I don't know what to say to you. It seems a long, long time since we really communicated, so I guess I shouldn't be surprised that you've chosen to slam the door in my face. Still, it hurts. You have a legitimate grievance—I can't deny that and I haven't tried to. Nor can I offer any excuses for myself. I did something I shouldn't have done. But it was a transitory something, utterly meaningless in the long run. I tried to tell you this. You weren't hearing me, though.

You should have been hearing me, Amelia. Hearing me and screaming at me and giving me the broad side of your tongue. Talking to me. Not denying that there was anything to talk about and gathering all your anger and hostility and sorrow and whatever into a tight little knot and locking it away. People who have a relationship talk to each

*other. I thought we had a relationship. Do we? I don't
know anymore.*

*When did things start to go wrong? More important,
why? I don't know. I know only that you've distanced yourself from me and put up barricades that I can't get through.*

*I want my wife back, Amelia. Don't make any hard and
fast decisions now. Take plenty of time, as much time as
you need. If you decide you want to make a real effort to
work things out, I'm here for you. Always. I think you
know that.*

All my love,
Gabriel

It was like reading a letter from a stranger. Amelia could even
admire the artistry with which Gabriel slithered from confession
to accusation. If only she could deny the charges, or at least feel
some small stirring of protest. Alas, she couldn't. It was as though
she had crossed a frontier and couldn't cross back. She was in a
world vastly different from the cozy, secure world she had inhabited for so long. Or thought she had inhabited. Whichever, it had
splintered around her. The new terrain was dark, wide open,
treacherous, and she didn't like it one damn bit.

She folded the letter and put it in her purse. Maybe a rereading
later, at a distance, would make it sound less smug. Maybe. She
wondered what kind of story Gabriel would tell (was perhaps already telling?) about her departure to cover his ass. No doubt she
could guess, if she put her mind to it. She preferred not to, knowing she wouldn't like it; also knowing she couldn't blame him.

Now it was time to go. Everything she was taking with her was
ready to be carried out to the car. It would fit easily. Of course she
had already shipped the bulkiest things, books and a trunk full of
winter clothes, to Jacqueline in New Jersey, but even so, she
wasn't taking much. Except for a few small household effects,
mostly pottery, she was leaving the house intact. Would she miss
it? Probably. After all, it represented a large chunk of her life. She
was suddenly glad she had given way to sentiment and had copies
of the Pilgrimage slides made. That was the part of her life with
Gabriel she would want to remember. Always.

Amelia walked to the door. Opened it. Closed it. Turned and went to the phone, picked up the receiver and punched out Suzanne's number.

"Hello." Suzanne sounded tired.

"It's me. I'm leaving Northvale."

"I know. Hal told me." Pause. "I meant to call to say good-bye, but I funked it."

"I almost did, too. I'm glad I didn't." Amelia's turn to hesitate. "I guess it's all over town."

"Have you ever known anything not to be?"

Amelia took a deep breath. "Gabriel's infidelities. Or am I kidding myself?"

"Amelia—"

"Don't you think you might have clued me in?"

"What would have been the point?"

What indeed? "Good-bye, Suzanne. Look after yourself."

"Yeah. You, too. Amelia—" One of Suzanne's deep, rattling breaths. "You know what Sara said when she heard about William? 'I guess I ought to feel something, Mom, but it all seems so remote. Like something that happened to somebody else.' "

Amelia winced. "You must be relieved."

"I suppose." A sigh. "She's young. The young can slough things off." Pause. "You're still young, Amelia."

"I'll be forty before the next blink. And I feel twice that."

"Think of what's ahead, not behind, and you'll manage. Good-bye, Amelia." The click was loud. And final.

Amelia hung up. She found that her legs were wobbly and had to sit down for a moment. Talking to Suzanne had churned all the horror up again. Now she had to wait for the turbulence to subside.

Up to now she had dealt with it reasonably well. Probably because she hadn't had to dwell long with doubt, uncertainty, fear of consequences. William Ellsworth's body had been discovered almost at once by a pair of weekend hikers from Maine. Shock traveled through Northvale like a tidal wave. Gabriel was devastated, and for a few days would talk about nothing but the fragility of life (monologues—Amelia was not required to contribute). The "Nuisance" ran an editorial denouncing illegal hunting and de-

180

manding stiffer penalties. The trustees of Northvale College and the alumni association decreed that flags on campus would fly at half-mast throughout the summer and the chapel bell would toll daily at 5 P.M. for a month. The memorial service for William Ellsworth was huge, as befitted someone who had been a college landmark for upwards of a quarter of a century, and had to be held in the theater, so it had been relatively easy for Amelia to avoid going one-on-one with anybody she knew.

As she had avoided going one-on-one with Suzanne since that night.

Oh yes, she had dealt with it reasonably well. Sure she had. By not really dealing with it at all. By devoting all her faculties to sorting things out with Gabriel and preparing for flight.

Whatever worked. It wasn't going to work forever, that was for sure. Down the road it would catch up with her. She wanted to be a long, long way down that road when it did.

Amelia stood up. Her legs felt okay. She was okay. Ready to go. She went out and brought the car around to the door. It took only a few minutes to load, and then everything that was going was out of the house except herself. She permitted herself a last look round from the doorway. The place looked much the same as usual, an open, airy space with a preponderance of rich wooden surfaces. Easy to get around in, easy to care for. It wouldn't miss her.

She walked through the door and closed it behind her and got into the car and drove down the hill. For the last time. She would, she told herself, stop the car at the bottom and look back.

But she found she was reluctant to look back. Because something might be gaining on her? Because she dreaded being turned into a pillar of salt?

Damned if she'd give way to the vapors now. She stopped the car and got out. There was the house perched on top of the hill. A very ordinary white frame house, a hill that was really only a sketch of a hill. No big deal, looking back. Nothing to seize up about.

Amelia got back into the car and drove away. One last swing through town to the highway, and she would put Northvale behind her.

She made that last swing (uneventful—no tugs at the heartstrings), but when she reached the end of Principle Street she didn't push on to the highway, she took the turning to the right. It was almost as if the car were driving itself.

If only she could simply drive away from the whole mess, relegate it to another life, like Sara Longman.

She couldn't. Heaven help her, but she couldn't.

The car that was driving itself approached Fricka McCardle's house, slowed down, stopped. The familiar white box with the bright blue trim looked small, diminished, faintly dingy. Amelia closed her eyes, remembering the memorial service for William Ellsworth. Remembering how she had sat with her eyes fixed resolutely on the stage while Nolan Neumeyer, president of Northvale College, colleagues in the English department (Gabriel included), a current student and a former student (both male), and a Northvale selectman delivered tributes, and while Andrea Jablonski of the music department sang Schubert's *Ave Maria;* how, joining the exodus, she had been unable to avoid the sight of Fricka McCardle, alone in a sea of empty seats, rigid and alabaster pale in a dress the color of weathered granite.

Amelia's nerve ends seemed to be on fire. She didn't want to be here. She wanted to start the engine again and drive away as fast as she could.

She got out of the car and walked up to the house, thinking that if ever a house needed a border of flowers, this one did. But the early blooms abounding elsewhere weren't in evidence here, only the odd sprig of yellow and a lot of tired-looking, stunted green shoots. Plainly Fricka had been neglecting her garden.

No one answered the doorbell. Amelia could have turned around and got back into the car and driven away. Instead, she walked around the side of the house to see if Fricka's car was parked in back. It was. She returned to the front door and rang the bell again. Rang and rang and rang, hearing the chimes merge in a blurred peal, and for good measure banged the knocker a couple of times.

The door opened. Slowly. Fricka McCardle stood in the doorway, eyes half closed, as if the light hurt them.

"Oh. It's you." No hint of welcome. No move to vacate the doorway.

Amelia took a deep breath. "May I come in? I need to talk to you."

It was painfully obvious that Fricka wanted to say no, but good manners were too deeply ingrained. "Of course." She stepped back, turned, and glided through the hall, tall and lean and almost spectral in a pale gray shirtwaist dress.

Amelia closed the door and followed Fricka into the parlor. The shades were drawn, and the room seemed to be steeped in twilight. Despite the poor visibility, Amelia could see the film of dust that dimmed the usually gleaming wooden surfaces, took the gloss from the myriad bits of china and glass. Fricka, too, appeared to be coated with dust. Or was it merely that she looked slightly disheveled? The overriding scent of lavender was a bit stale, a bit musty, and through it Amelia caught a whiff of something pungent, something earthy, something familiar—the moldering smell of age.

For a dizzying moment, time reeled backwards, and she was confronting Katherine Ellsworth again, smelling that smell.

Amelia wished she had never come. But of course she'd had no choice. She couldn't add uncertainty to the torments that would plague her for the foreseeable future. She had to know.

Plunge in. There was no other way. "I'm sure you must be wondering why I'm here. Or maybe not. It's about Katherine Ellsworth. I don't think she committed suicide. I think she was murdered."

No reaction. Clear blue eyes regarded her levelly. As if what she had said were of no importance. As if she were of no importance.

"I think you killed her, Fricka."

Still no reaction. The clear blue eyes remained level.

"Shortly after it happened—when I was too disoriented to register anything much—you referred to the cruelty of addressing the victim as 'Esquire.' Oh, you corrected it to 'Ms.' immediately, but I think you know the letter everybody thinks was sent to Katherine was really sent to William. How can you possibly know that, Fricka? The police don't. They never saw the envelope. But you did, didn't you?"

"Yes." The tone was flat, affectless. "It was addressed to him, but *she* opened it. She opened all his mail, you know. It was entirely by chance that I found that out. It was all by chance, really. I stopped by the house to pick up some seeds she'd ordered for me—she did that every year—and we were having coffee when the mail came. She simply grabbed the whole stack and started opening letters right in front of me, though I could see some were addressed to William. Then all of a sudden she started to laugh like a lunatic and passed the letter and the envelope across the table to me so I could share the joke. Some joke. Oh, I forced myself to smile, but I felt sick to my stomach. As soon as I could I excused myself—one of the advantages of age is that no one ever questions the demands of the bladder—and went to the bathroom and actually was sick. I ask you, what kind of a wife laughs when her husband is vilified? A miserable excuse for a wife, that's what kind. I'd always known it, of course, but having it brought home to me that way—

"I didn't really plan anything. It just happened. I opened the medicine cabinet to find mouthwash and I saw the bottle of pills and—Inspiration, I suppose. All at once I realized how much more pleasant William's life would be without Katherine. And I had the power to bring that about! I didn't hesitate. I used a handkerchief to open the bottle. I knew she would never taste anything—that black mud she brewed was so bitter. I asked her for a glass of water and as soon as her back was turned, I dropped the pills into her coffee. She drank it down to the last drop, yawned a couple of times, and went out like a light. I wrapped her fingers around the empty pill bottle—so the fingerprints would be fresh, you see—and left it on the table. It was so easy. I knew all I had to do was take away the envelope and everybody would assume the obvious. And they did. Not even William suspected the truth."

About that, Amelia wouldn't have placed any bets either way. William's quick liquidizing of assets by selling Katherine's desk and Katherine's porcelain could have meant preparation for flight from a woman who had killed to latch on to him and wasn't likely to let go without a struggle. On the other hand, it might have been simple greed, and he might have permitted Fricka to latch on to him for the same reason. Even the theory Amelia had once credited—before William denied having killed his wife at a moment when there was no reason for him to deny it and she had to ask herself "Who else?"—wasn't entirely out of the running: if he had been willing to kill her to preserve his nice, cushy existence, he might have been equally ready to take on a disposable wife to enhance it.

What a pair.

"Clever of you to figure it out, Amelia. Even if you did write the letters and had a head start because you knew it couldn't be suicide."

Amelia opened her mouth for the usual denial, closed it again. What was the use? What did it matter at this stage, anyway?

"It's really your fault, you see." Fricka sighed. "Would you believe that I haven't felt one iota of guilt over Katherine? I thought I surely would. I thought I would have lots and lots of sleepless nights, but I've been sleeping like a baby until— That woman had no conception of how lucky she was to have William all those years. He was such an extraordinary man. I sensed it the very first time I set eyes on him, and the years only confirmed it. So often I wished. . . . But of course it was quite impossible. He would never have left Katherine, no matter what. He was far too honorable. Oh, I know about the girls, if that's what you're wondering. I'll admit I was crushed when I found out. But I came to understand it and realize he wasn't to blame. *She* was. It would have been different with me. The bond between us was so deep, so true, nothing could break it. Our souls were one. We both knew that."

Amelia's stomach turned over. Familiar terrain, this. What woman has ever given her whole heart without thinking: "He's more myself than I am?" What man has ever come close to thinking it?

"I suppose you can't wait to shout the truth from the rooftops. I'll deny it, you know. I'll deny it till I'm blue in the face."

"I'm not going to tell anybody, Fricka. I just needed to know for my own peace of mind." The phrase reverberated. Hollow. Meaningless. What was peace of mind?

"On second thought, tell everybody. It doesn't matter anymore. Nothing matters anymore." Two tears, fat as beetles, crawled out of Fricka's eyes and down her cheeks. "I guess I'm being punished for killing Katherine. I guess the punishment fits the crime."

"I'm sorry."

Again the sense of uttering empty words. Sorry for whom? For Fricka the murderess? For William, who was prepared to kill rather than permit his life to be discommoded? For Katherine, who had mocked her husband in front of someone she knew worshiped him? For Suzanne? For herself?

Fricka didn't say anything. Just stood there, dry-eyed now, a fragile, spent old woman, a little dusty, like her house. Amelia had the impression of watching erosion happen in fast-forward.

She turned and walked out of the parlor and down the hall; let herself out; got into the Rabbit and drove away.